October Twilight

A Year in Paradise #10

Hildred Billings
BARACHOU PRESS

October Twilight

Copyright: Hildred Billings
Published: 10th October 2019
Publisher: Barachou Press

Chapter 1

SALLY

If her kids didn't shut the heck up, Sally was gonna slam on the brakes and turn that car around. She didn't care if they were halfway to the library. If Paige, Gage, Tucker, *and* the baby didn't get their acts together, this whole car was heading back to Florida Street.

"He's touching me!" Paige squirmed out of her seatbelt, elbow flying toward the baby's face. "Mom! Make him stop touching me!"

"It's a right mess back there." Tucker slid down the passenger seat beside his mother. A well-worn 3DS popped up in front of his face. "The natives are restless."

"Mom!"

"I ain't touchin' her!" Gage had the quietest voice in the family, but that only meant he screamed louder to be heard. "She's the one all up in my space!"

All up in my... Where had her six-year-old son learned a phrase like that? How out of touch was Sally that she had made it to forty-six and didn't remember when phrases like *"all up in my space"* became such common vernacular that little kids out in the sticks said them?

"Mom!"

Sally slammed on the breaks at the four-way stop separating Colorado Street from Sixth Street. She turned so quickly that her seatbelt pulled her against the driver's seat. The only reason her kids didn't laugh at the sight of Sally attempting to turn around and death-glare some sense into them was because they knew it would only make it worse.

"Gage Greenhill!" She wagged her finger in her son's face. Beside him, his twin sister kept a snicker behind her hand. Oh, she wasn't getting away with her noise, either. The only one getting away with anything was baby Daisy, and that was because she was barely over a year old. Anyone still in a child seat probably didn't understand reason very well. "You leave your sister alone, young man. Remember what your other mom and I said about respecting boundaries and personal space? I don't care how small this car is or how big you're getting. There are ways to sit next to your siblings without making them uncomfortable!" Her finger moved toward Paige, who had fallen into a fit of giggles that made her light brown braid fall in front of her face. "As for you, missy, you need to realize that your brother ain't gonna get out of touching you when we're all packed in here like sardines. Now, if he's going out of his way to mess with you, that's one thing..."

"He was totally..."

"Was he putting his hand on your leg? No? I can't stop his leg from rubbing up against yours. Maybe if we get a new car..."

Before Sally could get too wistful about things beyond her financial range, someone honked their horn behind her.

"Shit!" Sally pressed the gas pedal and cruised through the four-way stop. She had missed her turn about three times, and the person behind her was *not* happy about the hold-up.

Too bad she hadn't looked both ways before crossing the intersection.

"Whoa!" Tucker dropped his 3DS onto the floor of the front seat. The momentum of the car was in full throttle as Sally sailed down Colorado Street before another car had the chance to T-bone them. Wild honks sounded in the distance. A man shouted in their direction. Sally hoped to God that he didn't see the bumper sticker affiliating her with Paradise Valley's only full-time law enforcement officer.

The car quieted as they continued down Colorado Street. Houses passed. Trucks and cars parallel parked along the sidewalk turned into blurs. Although her heart calmed down, Sally kept her teeth clamped and her eyes glued onto the road before them. She was supposed to turn left back at the intersection and swing onto Main Street, the fastest way to get to the library.

Unfortunately, she was so rattled from what happened that she almost missed her next turn.

"Heh..." Gage snickered. "Mom said a bad word."

Thankfully, that was all anyone said the rest of the way to the library.

They were lucky that Paradise Valley Public Library was open on Saturdays, albeit for much shorter hours. They were not as lucky that the weekend shift had been picked up by the head librarian (and the only one to get a decent wage around there) who always made a big deal about the Greenhills rolling through the door and ransacking the children's section.

Sally only wanted to put down her bag at one of the community tables and rock her baby in her carrier. The twins were old enough to pick out books for themselves, and Tucker would either grab some Hardy Boy mysteries or pretend nobody saw him poke through Babysitter's Club collections over on the "girl's" side. *I like the drama,* he once told his parents, who didn't say anything disparaging about his reading choices but were certainly intrigued by them. *"Girls get the best drama in their books! Like those shows you watch, Ma!"*

That would have been asking for the world to offer a small kindness. The library was crowded that Saturday. Too crowded for the three older Greenhill kids to own the children's section. The community college students commandeered the big tables. The Stephen King book club dominated the back room. A few other mothers had brought their kids to check out some books. Or maybe they were looking for free babysitting while they ran down to the store.

No matter what, the Greenhills appearing was the final straw for librarian Yi.

"Oh, no." She dropped a stack of books she had been returning to the cookbook section. "Watch out for that little boy's hands! Last time he went through the picture books, he left them all sticky! I had to clean and *clean!*"

Everyone in the library, including the adults with their headphones on, turned to look at Gage and his mother. Gage had a particular habit whenever he came to the library. One that

Sally had completely forgotten about in her exhaustion.

The boy loved his little peppermint candies. That in itself wasn't an issue – although Sally had been struggling to get him to cut back, for his teeth's sake – but it was what he *did* with the candy that drove everyone crazy.

When he wasn't gnashing them with his front teeth, lips wide open, of course, he was pulling them out of his mouth. Those sticky fingers soon ended up on every surface around him, from counters to books on the library shelves.

"Gage," Sally said, elbow slumped against the table. Beside her, Frankie Delacour's brother, a young man named Dominic, pretended to not notice the baby plopped down in front of him. "Please don't eat your candy when in the library. You and your sister need to go wash your hands in the bathroom first, anyway." Probably for the best. Sally had no idea where those hands had been in the morning while she tended to the garden and made lunch. The twins followed her everywhere. If she were in the garden, they were hunting for worms. If she were inside, they were throwing their toys around and poking through the garbage "looking for treasures." During the calm of the day, Sally would sit back and think that nothing truly made her happier than having four kids in rural America.

Then she would drag their asses into town and ended up wondering if she could wipe them from existence!

Tucker minded his business in the YA section while the twins ran off to the bathroom. Sally closed her eyes and tried not to fall asleep. She wouldn't have the luxury, anyway. As soon as she heaved a sigh of quiet relief, she heard the screams of a pair of twins up to no good.

"What the..." Yi snapped her head toward Sally. "What are they doing in there? I just cleaned those bathrooms!"

Sally dragged herself out of the chair, leaving her baby behind on the table. She forgot about Daisy until she was in front of the men's bathroom – because of course both went in – beholding the mischief.

"Look!" Paige shoved her brother aside and stuck both of her hands into the bottom of the men's urinal. "It makes a mess!"

It sure did.

***

The shopping cart ambled down the aisles of Paradise Valley's only decent supermarket. Fluorescent lights buzzed. The clattering of carts and wheelchairs pounded into the earth. People having loud conversations sputtered out their "reckons" and 'dang-nabbits." Jars of spaghetti sauce banged against the floor.

Ah, that last one was technically Sally's fault.

Because she was in charge of those darn kids getting rowdy in the pasta aisle. Of course it was her kids. Paige and Gage had apparently snuck into the family's supply of sugar that morning. It was the only explanation for them hanging from the rafters and whooping like two crazy hellions straight from the demon himself.

The worst thing about the twins when they got this way was how they influenced their big brother. Tucker put on a good show of acting older than he was at nearly-nine, but his age still made him susceptible to childish tomfoolery. When Paige and Gage started chasing each other up and down the bread aisle and threw oranges in the produce section, he was as likely to tell them to knock it off as he was to join in – until Sally found out, anyway. That was the major difference between her oldest and the twins. Tucker was born with an innate sense of guilt. The twins were in their own world of gassing each other up before eventually turning on one another. Sally had no idea what Daisy would be like when she finally joined their ranks of playtime. She didn't want to know.

Right now, Tucker looked between the oranges and peaches. After all, his mother hadn't said anything yet, and the twins were having a blast pressing their thumbs into the hard skin of the oranges. It wasn't until Sally rolled up and narrowed her eyes at Tucker that he finally swung around and barked at the twins to pull themselves together.

"Thanks." Sally grabbed one of her reusable produce bags and sifted through the cauliflower heads. "You're a big, help, Tu..."

"Can I get a donut?"

Ah, yes. He wanted a reward for keeping the family out of trouble. If it were only the two of them, Sally would indulge her oldest with a donut. Yet in the company of the twins, who heard the word *donut,* Sally couldn't condone giving her children any more sugar.

Which, of course, started a protest of whiny kids around her shopping cart.

God, I wish Candace were here... For all Sally knew, her wife was off responding to a call about a violent offender at the local Pump 'N' Go. *Some days are like that...* As the only deputy around, Candace spent most of her days at the tiny police station filling out reports, dealing with drunks in lockup, and responding to the occasional traffic accident and report of tomfoolery that extended beyond her kids throwing oranges at the store. But that's what made her such a good parent! Candace had the voice and the authoritative presence to make everyone, including her kids, listen. And she did it without threatening anyone!

She ain't here, 'cause she's gotta pay for us. Remember, Sal, this is your role in this family. The caregiver. The cook and cleaner. The laundry folder. The personal driver. The one who showed up to school board and PTA meetings to make sure her four kids got a decent education in their corner of the county. Candace was about the meta of Paradise Valley. She protected her community, which meant protecting her family. Sally? She took care of their family. These four kids and the wife she saw a couple hours a day were her whole world.

Which meant that she took all the flack when the Greenhill kids went off the deep end.

She managed to keep herself together long enough to put the dinner groceries in her cart and roll the troops up to the only opened lane. Busybody Anem Singer was on duty, and the first thing she asked Sally as she started ringing up produce was, "Hey, Sal! How you doin'?"

That was the moment Daisy decided to speak. Not only did she utter a sound, but she let rip a loud, curdling cry that demanded naptime. Now.

Sally slapped down her wallet and looked Anem in the eye.

"How do you think I'm doing?"

Chapter 2

CANDACE

They were on their third pot of coffee for the day. Not a record, but close enough that Candace seriously questioned whether she would get any sleep that night.

Then again, she didn't usually come into the station on the weekends, unless there was something bad enough going on around town. One of the things that most appealed to her about being promoted to deputy a few years ago was the more stable schedule. Granted, law enforcement wasn't the career for those looking for a ho-hum 9-5 that let them punch out at the hour and go home for another sixteen. Candace had spent as many Sunday mornings in the station as she had Wednesday nights, mostly because of a drunk driver making a reckless fool of themselves all over *her* roads.

Three pots of coffee in as many hours? It was *that* kind of day.

"So let me get this straight." Sheriff Peterson, the only man in the county who knew how to knock Candace back down to *Yes, Sirs* and *No, Sirs,* pinched the bridge of his nose and flipped over the last piece of paper to cross the table. "The boy is saying he's part of a little ring of arsonists, but oh, we're not supposed to ask any questions beyond what *he's* done? I can't deal with this." He held out his empty cup. "These damn Millennials are too freakin' much for me."

That coffee cup was Candace's cue to get up and refill it again. She might as well freshen up her cup as well. Wasn't like she forgot that Peterson wanted cream *and* sugar in his. The man had a sweet tooth that was only matched by his love for lactose. "That's what the

Musgrave kid is saying. He cops to the last fire, but he claims that he's only responsible for two of the six this past year." She didn't touch the Millennial comment. Candace wasn't hip on her generation names – hell, she didn't know what she was, either! Was she a Gen-Xer or a Boomer? Who kept track of these things? – but she was pretty sure the high schoolers were now some new, young, hip generation. What was it. Gen Z? J? B? Shoot, she could barely remember her ABCs now that she was strung out on caffeine. "He hasn't given us any names for the others, though. He claims that if he 'snitches' he's gonna get 'stitches.' Thought he was all bluff until we really started pushing him to give us some names. Boy was crying and saying that they weren't from around here. Some 'bad guys' he said. Wanted us to think they were out of Portland. Some hoods or gang bangers, I dunno. This is giving me a headache, too."

The whole summer had given Deputy Candace Greenhill a headache, albeit for different reasons than before. Last summer, she had raging migraines from the wildfire smoke coming from every direction. *Got so bad that the fire marshal was talking about possible evacuations.* Luckily, people were so uptight over the possibility of their homes going up in flames that they more or less behaved themselves, giving Candace a chance to do her own preparations should evacuations be on the docket. This summer, though? Arsons!

They couldn't get through a whole fortnight without somebody's barn going up in smoke. The fire marshal dragged so much ass with his investigations that, by the time he realized these were intentional fires and not accidents, it was too late. The firebugs were given free rein to destroy structures and kill some livestock. Law enforcement thought they caught a break the last time, though. Two girls were found around the site, and one was not helped by the rumors surrounding her. Instead of taking the fall, however, a confession from the girl's cousin revealed the truth.

About that fire, anyway.

Now, Dillon Musgrave was under house arrest with his electronics confiscated and his reputation around town utterly ruined. Candace hated it had to be that way, but when bad eggs began to stink, they had to be tossed.

That didn't mean she thought the boy beyond help, but the most important thing was keeping him watched and segregated from the people urging him to commit acts of arson. It also didn't explain how these supposed kids from Portland were driving all the way to Paradise Valley to set some fires. Didn't they have tons of flammable stuff in Portland to light on fire? And make it *Portland's* problem?

Paradise Valley wasn't exactly rich with human resources. Aside from Candace, there were a couple officers who made the rounds, but for the most part, it was only her – and Peterson, she supposed, but he jaunted all over the whole county, sometimes in a single day. *She* was in charge of Paradise Valley. This was *her* town. If she couldn't control her town, then what good was she to the sheriff's department?

Sometimes Candace longed for the structure of big city police stations, but then she remembered it meant working with more numbskulls and answering to more dunderheads, and she was fine with the several hundred that called Paradise Valley their home.

"The kid's gotta talk," Peterson said with a shrug. He didn't thank Candace for the coffee. "That's all there is to it. We don't have much evidence to go off outside of his confession. The witnesses are sketchy at best." He referred to Leigh-Ann Hardy, Carrie Sage, and Christina Rath, three high-school girls who were already up to way too much trouble in their senior year. *I saw both Leigh-Ann and Christina grow up around here.* Carrie was brand-new to town. Candace kicked herself for believing the rumors about the troublemaking "Rolltide Ruffian" as some had taken to calling her, due to her Alabaman origins. Turned out the closest Carrie had come to involvement was living in the same house as the perpetrator. "What has the mayor's daughter been saying?"

Candace sighed, not because she didn't want to talk about Christina, but because she *still* couldn't believe that the mayor's daughter was wrapped up in something like this. *She's a bit of a moody teen, of course, but you'd think she'd have more common sense after seeing what her mother puts up with.* Mayor Rath wasn't new. She had been the mayor for seven years. Or was it more by now? Either way, it was most of Christina's life. She knew better!

"She's the worst witness, if you ask me. According to everyone, including the Musgrave boy, she had just started dating him a couple of days before. The statements corroborate. Dillon Musgrave told her he had something cool to show her, they drove out to the Connors' land, and before Christina knew what was happening, he lit the whole thing on fire. No accelerant."

"No accelerant! How did it burn so quickly?"

"Like it says in the marshal's report," Candace said with a nod to one of the stacks of paper, "the structure was old and hardly sound. There was enough termite rot in there to bring the whole thing down eventually. We're lucky we haven't had kids crushed to death in some of the barns around here."

"What were those other girls doing, huh? Absolutely no good, in a town like this."

Candace pretended she hadn't heard that. Like many of the old guard around the county, some only put on airs that they "tolerated" the queer contingent. Paradise Valley had a long and varied history as a lesbian commune-turned "real" small town, but there were still those from other parts that turned their noses and spoke with a sneer. Candace had lived there most of her life. She was used to it. That didn't mean she indulged it.

"The other girls confess to a little nookie, yeah." Candace could hardly say that without laughing. *Like I can talk! What do you think I was doing at that age? Making love in a mansion?* Everyone, and that meant *everyone,* knew that if you were a teenager who wanted some private time with your girl, you found yourselves an empty barn for an hour or two. More comfortable than necking in the backseat of a car. *We're not supposed to let them do it, but most farmers look the other way as long as they're not causing any problems.* That had been the silent agreement until Dillon Musgrave and his buddies ruined everything that past summer. Six barns gone in nearly as many weeks. Go figure! *I might have lost my own virginity in one of those barns...*

"Nookie." Peterson scoffed. "That's one way to put it. Well, can't stop kids from having their fun, but we have to round up these other firebugs before they burn down this whole town. Who knows? Maybe they'll take their fun to another town and be *their* problem for a change."

"As long as it's not in your county, right?"

"Damn right."

Candace sipped her coffee. The buzz continued to throb in her veins. "Maybe it's time we call in some help, Sheriff. If they're from Portland, then this goes beyond us, anyway."

"To hell with that. I don't care if they're from Portland or Timbuktu, if they're committing crimes in *my* county, I want to take care of them myself. You know what those Portland boys do? They roll through like they down the damn place. That's assuming you can convince someone to get their asses down here! They're stretched thinner than we are. Do you know how many times I've asked for another officer in our ranks? Can you imagine if I had a proper detective for once?"

"I know I don't look like Sherlock Holmes, sir, but I'm not too bad at puzzling things out." Candace hoped he knew. They had been working together for as long as she had a badge.

"You want to take responsibility for this case, Greenhill?"

"Now, I didn't say that..."

Peterson snorted into his coffee. "Between this mess and the serial flasher over in Erin's Drop, I'm having a helluva year. Except that flasher isn't destroying property and acting a proper menace. Just landing himself on the sex offenders' list."

Candace's cell phone rang. She was about to send it to voicemail when she saw her wife's name. "One second, sir," she said. "I have to take this."

He waved her off as she stepped away. Candace didn't have a chance to greet her wife, however. Sally was already on it.

"When are you coming home?"

Candace had to stop and collect her bearings. "Hopefully soon, hon. We're kinda tied up here investigatin' the arsons."

"Come home soon, for the love of God. The kids are driving me nuts and they really need their other mom to run them breathless so I can get dinner started."

"I..."

"*Please,* Candy. I'm going nuts! Do you know what they were doing in the store? Throwing oranges! We'll be lucky if I'm ever allowed to shop there again!"

Five minutes later, Candace returned to the table, where her boss finished his coffee.

"What your kids do this time?" he asked.

"Something about throwing oranges."

"Better than apples, I guess."

Candace sat down. Instead of mulling over her own children's actions, she focused on the misdeeds and issues of other's.

Chapter 3

SALLY

The kids did not go to bed quietly. One would have thought that, after tearing up half the town and eating a large dinner of carbs, the twins would have fallen asleep on the couch long before they made it to their baths. The baby was the only one who conked out as soon as Sally put her down. Tucker begged to stay up an hour later since it was Saturday night and he wanted to finish a movie on TV, but Candace hit the "Record" button on the remote and told him it would be waiting for him the next day. He knew the drill: he couldn't stay up later on the weekends until he was ten. Only a little over a year to go for the resident third grader.

Aside from giving the final word on their son's going to bed, Candace's big contribution to bedtime was checking in on the twins to give them kisses. By then, they had already been bathed, dressed in their PJs, and dragged to bed by the birth giver. *Me. That's me. I'm the one who carried these kids and squeezed them out of my hoo-ha!* Candace had paid for the honor, much like she paid for everything around there, but in the true fashion of a parenting-dichotomy, she got the "easy" part of managing their behavior.

"Sorry to hear they were such hellions today." Candace slumped on the edge of the bed, the mattress sagging beneath her muscular body. "Must be that change-of-season feeling. People act really weird around this time of year, especially those that don't know how to control their behavior so well. Kinda amazing we haven't had a bunch of arrests lately. Usually, I've got at least two people in lockup by early October."

Sally climbed out of her flannel pants and reveled in standing in front of the oscillating fan in the corner of the room. The backs of her sweaty thighs demanded some moisture-free reprieves before they finally hit the shower. *I get a whole ten minutes of hot water by this time.* Hardly enough time to properly bathe after a long day of child-wrangling and errand-running. *I'm going to bed stinky. That's all there is to it.* Candace hit the shower as soon as she came home. Then the kids took their turns, including a rush for the baby as Sally held her head out the bathroom door and yelled at Candace to check on dinner. The garlic breadsticks were half-burnt because Candace hadn't heard her.

"The kids act like that all the time," she said, turning to her wife to dry off the backs of her thighs. "The older the twins get, the more ramped up they get. You ask me, they've completely realized that they're different genders and are internalizin' that our culture expects them to treat each other differently because of it!"

"What are you on about?" Candace pulled on her house socks, the ones with the little nubs on the bottom that kept her from slipping on the hardwood floors. Their Victorian-inspired house on Florida Street was purchased with all the original fixings, including hardwood floors, wood stove, and brick fireplace. They had planned on putting in some cozy carpeting before Tucker was born. After his appearance, however, they were grateful to have such easy-to-clean flooring. Toddler-Tucker threw up. A lot. "They're kids! The only thing they're internalizing is their hunger for more tussling. I'm telling you, Paige is gonna be a helluva track star one day. Maybe cross-country, if we get her outside more. Dunno about Gage yet. Clark High has really revitalized the co-ed soccer program in recent years. I should start kicking the ball around with them more often..."

Sally rolled her eyes. She loved her wife. *Truly,* she did. Candace was the epitome of good people. She was as strict as she was soft-hearted when it came to dealing with messes, be they the townsfolk getting into trouble, or their own kids banging each other's heads into the wall. She was good with money and wasn't afraid to ask for promotions and raises – or, Heaven forbid, better benefits for her family. She had proposed to Sally by taking her hand on the sidewalk and declaring, *"There is no one I want to make a family with more than you, Sally Reynolds. Be my wife, and let's do this thing."*

Candace had her frustrating sides, of course. She was a single-minded woman. Some would say that made her *simple,* but that was an insult to her overall intelligence. *You have to be single-minded doing her job, I guess.* Focus. That's what it was called. Candace could turn on her tunnel vision as easily as she turned on the sirens to her cruiser when she saw a drunk driver weaving across Main Street. (Which happened more than the sheriff's office wanted to admit.) Yet what good was that when Sally tried to tell her what was going on with their kids? When she said, *"They're internalizing shitty gender norms,"* she meant that the twins had gone from playing with the same toys to Gage declaring he didn't want to touch a Barbie again. Which greatly upset Paige, who was counting on him to help in the Barbie Doll Hair Salon last week.

It was inevitable. Sally knew this, because she saw the way kids played with each other. She saw the cartoons they watched and heard what the other parents told their own children. For every mom who said, *"There's no difference between pink and blue, Johnny! Just be you!"* there was another who totally rolled over when the mother-in-law screeched that Johnny should never, *ever* play house!

Did Candace see that, though? She saw some of the end products when she rounded up rowdy teens at the overlooks, or when they went to high school softball games where some of the boys still made fun of the star female players for "throwing like girls." Granted, with Clark High's championship team, that meant a softball to an asshole's face...

"I'm so tired." Sally shuffled toward the bathroom, her underwear sagging against her thighs and her pullover drooping against her shoulders. "I don't know what I'm gonna do once the baby is running around."

"Tucker is all about minding the others. He's gonna take over your job one day!"

Sighing, Sally slumped against the bathroom door. "He's not gonna be interested in that once he's a little older, and right now the twins are as likely to get him wrapped up in mischief as he is to tell them to knock it off. Plus, the twins are getting good at undermining authority. Even their kindergarten teacher has told me that..."

"What do the teachers around here know about twins, huh?" Candace scoffed, her body hitting the bed. "How many of them do they get, *hm?* Like one pair every generation? Get outta here. Twins have different dynamics. They got their own language."

"They get plenty of twins in an IVF-town like this one, Candy. There's a pair of twins in Tucker's class."

"Really?"

"Really. Triplets in the middle school. Gay moms who used IVF. It's the new age."

"Huh."

Sally finally took off her sweater and tossed it into the hamper across the room. She missed, and the fabric crumpled against the wall.

"By the way," she continued, "we need to talk about the party next weekend."

She heard Candace sighing all the way in the other room. "I told you I'd get the day off, promise! Peterson knows it's the twins' birthday!"

Sally turned on the shower. The water was cold, although she cranked up the *hot*. *This is what I get for going last in a family of six.* "It's not only about you gettin' the day off. I need to make sure I've got all the ingredients for the cake! That means going to Wal-Mart and gettin' some pans, because I gotta make them some Falcon fighter or whatever it is from Star Wars!"

"Millennium Falcon?"

Sally threw her bra out the bathroom door. "Yeah, the Harrison Ford and Chewie thing." She could *feel* Candace shuddering in the bedroom. The woman was enthralled when *A*

New Hope came out, and she cried when Disney brought a new trilogy for their kids to grow up on.

The hot water finally arrived. As soon as she felt it, Sally leaped into the shower. Instead of waiting for her shower to end before continuing their conversation, she yelled her side.

"Can you go online and find us a pinata from Star Wars? I tried looking for some on Amazon the other day but didn't know what was actually Star Wars or the other Star thing."

"The *other* star thing?" Candace shouted back, voice carrying through glass walls.

"You know what I mean! The thing with Spock!"

"How the hell did I end up in a marriage with you, woman? Can't keep your Star Wars and your Star Trek apart!"

"I ain't talkin' about no Star Trek!"

"You just were!"

Sally snatched her bar of soap off its ledge. "Could you *please* help get some stuff for the birthday party? I'm gonna be up to my ass in sequins making their Halloween costumes! You ain't gonna be around on Halloween so I have to do all that myself." Her anxiety peaked from thinking about it. At least Halloween was understandable. Candace worked nonstop on that day. When the kids weren't pulling vandalistic pranks, the adults were drinking too much and getting behind the wheels of their cars.

Except that meant Sally needed help with the twins' party. Candace wasn't completely absolved from menial parenting tasks because she worked a tough job. She could get out a *couple* times of year, like for Halloween and St. Patrick's Day, but she better put in the time in between!

"I will take care of it, don't worry!"

Sally barely had time to rinse off the soap before the cold water hit. She hurried to turn off the shower before she started shaking. Only then did she realize she forgot a towel.

"I'm gonna make you a list," she insisted, as soon as she saw Candace lying across their bed. Sally stepped into the bedroom, naked and wet, and fished for a towel from the hamper. I plan on heading to Wal-Mart around Wednesday while the kids are at school and I only got the baby to worry about, so…"

"Yeah, no worries."

"I'm serious." Sally wrapped the towel around her and flopped down next to her wife. "I'm up to my ass in kid crap. When Daisy starts running around, I… I dunno what I'm gonna do. I'm not getting any younger. I'm already winded by the time we leave the store. I…"

Should she say it? Should she say what she had been thinking for the past few months?

"I'm starting to wonder if having a fourth baby was the right thing to do."

"Now, now…" Candace turned toward her, that graying hair making her look an age older. "You said so yourself when we decided to have one more baby. You said that you could handle it, and that God told you it was the right thing to do. You always wanted four kids, Sal. I've always been on board with four and no more."

Lord, it always tickled her that it rhymed…

"It's gonna be fine. You took care of twin toddlers, you can take care of one more."

At least she didn't say, *"You kinda signed up for it, and she's here now, so do it."* That's what Sally told herself when she stared at her know-it-all son, her wild-thing twins, and her screaming baby. Half the town ran in the other direction when they approached. Sally barely noticed it anymore.

Did Candace know how bad it got sometimes?

No, she had to stop thinking like that. Candace had a tough, dangerous job that paid their bills and allowed Sally to stay home and have her dream existence. *Dreams aren't always rosy, though. They're always work. You gotta keep working.* Maybe it wouldn't be too bad. Tucker would get more mature with age and take up the mantle of strong, big brother. The twins would mellow out when they reached grade school. Everyone was so used to babies now that Daisy was hardly a problem. The worst they had to worry about was her being too spoiled!

We are a unit. We have our roles. This is how it works. Even though Sally was exhausted. Even though it felt like the whole weight of the family was on her shoulders. Even though there were people in that town who saw Candace more than her own family did. Even though people gave Sally crap for the behavior of her children, not that she could do much more than she already did.

Even though she worried. She always worried.

Oh, she didn't have time to worry! She had birthday cakes to make, invitations to respond to, and goodie bags to put together! She had Halloween costumes to sew and candy to buy for the trick-or-treaters they never saw.

She had dinners to make and laundry to wash. She had groceries to buy and cars to refuel.

She had bills to pay with money she didn't make.

Good thing she put so much emphasis on making this family work and dying with this woman alongside her. Because Sally didn't have any other choices. She was well into her forties with four kids and no money of her own.

Candace pulled her into an unsolicited embrace. At first, Sally almost told her to keep her hands to herself. When she realized it wasn't a sexual advance, she wrapped her arms back around Candace's torso and sighed.

Wasn't it amazing what the simplest of gestures could do for her anxiety?

Chapter 4

CANDACE

The station didn't usually get so much uniformed traffic, outside of the biannual county meetings and the occasional high-profile perp in lockup.

There were no perps, currently. No meetings. Only a meeting of the fire and law enforcement minds as one told the other how to do their jobs.

"The way I see it," Adam Trough, the county fire marshal who was in charge of the arsonist investigations, said, "we're not getting anywhere with the Musgrave kid. Short of the county DA throwing the book at him, we either have to let it go or wait for his so-called buddies to attack again." Before either Candace or Peterson could jump on him, he continued, "How many old barns are left in this whole county? Two? Now that it's raining every day, we might as well admit that they're done. This time next year, they'll have either moved on to crispier pastures or..."

"You seriously want to roll over?" Candace interrupted, the sheriff sucking in his breath over her outburst. "Let me at that kid and I'll have him shitting his pants while calling for his mama." She knew Mrs. Musgrave well enough. She knew how to get to that woman's boy.

"I didn't say anything about *rolling over,*" Adam said. "I said that we needed to be careful about how we managed our resources. I'm only one man, for Christ's sake. You want me expending more time on this, I'm gonna need help. Meanwhile, I've got housefires, car fires, and industrial kitchen fires every other week! Do you know how many open investigations I have?"

The law enforcement contingency were silent, waiting.

"Three! That's not including the barn fire arsons!"

Three. A whole three investigations. Wow. Amazing. *Meanwhile, I'm backed up with a meth lab in Roundabout and a couple of kids street racing on the highway around midnight.* This man wanted to talk about resources? They could start with how understaffed the sheriff's office was! That was the whole point of this joint investigation. Three heads were better than one, especially if that one head was Adam Trough, a man who couldn't rub his belly and pat his head at the same time. *How he got to be fire marshal, I'll never know.* Candace could do a better job than him at this rate.

"Give me the kid," Candace repeated. "I'll figure out who is helping him set those fires. The *last* thing we should do is roll over and pretend this never happened! What the hell are we, anyway? Are we the protectors of this town, or are we a bunch of ninnies who don't know our asses from our elbows? What will people say if they found out we dropped the investigation?"

Peterson shook his head. "People are gonna say what they say. Although I do agree that we shouldn't completely give up at this point, although the trail is cold. I'd rather bring in an outside investigator to help than..."

"Great. Yeah. Bring in the city boys," Adam said with a snort. "I'm sure they don't have better things to do than root through Portland's hobo campfires."

He laughed, but both Candace and Peterson had thoroughly discussed the pros and cons of turning this over to Multnomah County investigators. Not only were they also understaffed – and overburdened – but without conclusive evidence that one of their citizens was involved, they were likely to laugh Paradise Valley out of the urban area.

"Give me the kid," Candace repeated. "I know him. I know his mother. He may not like me much, but he'll open up to me more than some stranger from Portland."

"Speaking of the kids..." Adam tapped his finger against his lip. Already, Candace knew this was going somewhere else. "We need to go over the fire safety and first-aid course at the school this week."

While that *was* an order of business during this meeting, it was the kind of thing that could easily be coordinated over email. Candace knitted her brows into a tight knot, looked Adam in the eye, and said, "We can talk about that later. Right now is about the Musgrave kid."

"What's the point if we're letting more Musgrave kids get made out there? We need to make sure these kids know that there won't be any more fires on our watch. You want to scare some sense into the kids of Paradise Valley?" That was directed at Candace. "Then let's get them at the assembly."

Could Candace convey any more of her disgust? How like this little weasel to shift to something he had more control over, as if that made him the big man in the county! *One of these days I'm gonna totally snap. Snap his back in half, that is.* She could do it, too. Candace was bigger than anyone in the room, and that included Peterson.

"The assembly won't mean a damn thing if they're laughing behind our backs," Candace said. "Are you kidding me? Do you know anything about high schoolers? They're ruthless little bastards who are big enough to start serious trouble but don't have the brain development to know when to quit." Harsh, but Candace had seen most of the crap kids got up to like she had a front-row seat. Before she was an honored deputy of the town, she had been the head Clark High School lunch lady. Every day, Monday through Friday, she served entrees to the ungrateful spawn of the county's east side. Oh, sure, kids were great in their own special way, but when a woman worked around them every day for several years, she had seen and heard everything. Things their own parents hadn't heard. She was old enough and experienced enough to have seen some of the great relationship blowups like she had bought tickets for the events. *Ask me what I think about Mikaiya Marcott and Ariana Mura. You wanna talk about feeling old?* She had been there when those two gangly teens started going out ten years ago! She had seen the breakup. Saw them get back together almost a whole year ago. Because it wasn't enough that Candace arrived to car crash scenes where the likes of Ariana, who used to be so girly and scrawny, hauled victims into an ambulance, sometimes with her own big, bulky arms.

Meanwhile, Candace felt like the same exact person she had been fifteen years ago, when she was slinging mashed potatoes and coleslaw onto plastic trays. Remembering that she had come so far into her dream job blew her mind. In fifteen years, she had not only changed careers, but gotten married and had four kids. *I barely knew who Sally was when I was a lunch lady.* These two gentlemen in their uniforms hadn't known her as anyone but Officer Candace Greenhill, a later-in-life recruit who quickly became a town favorite until she was unanimously recommended for the role of town deputy. She may or may not have thought about gunning for sheriff whenever Peterson retired. Granted, that was an elected role, but nobody went against the incumbent.

She really wished she were the sheriff right now. Peterson should be directing this meeting and making Adam see the idiocy of his statements. Adam didn't have legal authority to make arrests, only conduct investigations. He required the aid of the sheriff's office. He needed them more then they needed him!

"You want to make a difference with kids?" Candace continued with a grunt in her throat. "You make sure that they know what is and isn't acceptable. You make it clear that this isn't about bossing them around and making them shit their pants for the fun of it. We've got their families and their friends to protect. We've got their future kids to protect. It's not about snitching and not about being a lame-o. It's about letting them be kids without worry they'll be fooling around in a barn that's about to go up in smoke!"

Peterson shook his head. "Yes, the real important thing here is that we preserve their make-out barns..."

He totally missed the point, huh? Candace almost smacked her head against the table, but

Adam finally said, "You're right. Sorry. We still need to talk about the assembly, though. I've already had a chat with the fire department, and while they do their demonstrations, I want you guys to have a long chat with the audience about the importance of keeping things safe and chugging along. You do it however you see fit. I'm sure the principal and the superintendent won't have any issues with us getting to the bottom of which of the devils are about to light their houses on fire."

"In the meantime," Candace cut in, "I want the Musgrave kid in the interview room."

That was mostly for the sheriff to know. He was the only one with the authority to put Dillon Musgrave in the interview room, and he would undoubtedly want to take part in whatever Candace had up her sleeve. *That's fine. He can watch and give all the critiques he wants.* Sometimes, Sally told Candace that she was "one-track minded." That she indulged in a little too much tunnel vision thanks to her job. That sure was the truth, now wasn't it? But where Sally said it like it was something to improve upon, Candace embraced it. That tunnel vision was what helped her keep her focus when times were tough and the tough got going. *I'll be damned if I let a group of organized firebugs go on my watch.* She didn't want one guilty kid. She wanted *all* of them.

Only then would she be able to sleep at night. Because right now, she spent an awful lot of time fretting that her own children would wake up to the smell of smoke and kiss of fire on their cheeks.

The more she thought about her family, the more she thought about putting the masterminds of the arsons behind bars.

Chapter 5

SALLY

Moms with short haircuts and fuzzy cardigans wrapped around their bodies crammed into the hard, plastic chairs of Clark High School's library. *This has got to be the biggest PTA turnout in five years!* Not since those rumors of party drugs going around the school had Sally seen so many moms, dads, and concerned grandparents in one tiny high school library. Usually, they couldn't fill the five rows of plastic chairs if they paid people to attend.

Tonight, however, Sally had to squeeze her glutes and hope she didn't accidentally rub a thigh against her neighbor. She stuffed her purse into her lap and folded her hands through the strap loops, her nearest neighbor scoffing at the frizzy brown hair touching her cheek. *I can't help it, now can I!* The static was unreal that night. Lightning storm was supposed to light the sky up, and whenever electricity was in the air, Sally's hair took over the place.

She was lucky she didn't have any of the kids with her. Candace was home with them, a fact that both relieved Sally and gave her a taste of petty revenge. *She has to feed them dinner, get them washed, and put them to bed – all by herself!* Oh, Candace was perfectly capable. She simply didn't have to do it that often. Every time Sally thought about it, her mouth twitched into another diabolical smile. *I hadn't changed the baby's diaper yet! Have fun, Candy!*

Oh, this would have been a terrible environment for the baby, especially this late in the evening. With energy high and concerned parents flooding the meeting, Sally felt less petty toward Candace and more worried about the state of the world.

"Hey, everyone! Please take your seats!" Greta Williams, the PTA president with a kid in every public school around, stood up from her seat and waved a small rainbow flag above her head. Flanking her were the vice president and the treasurer, two women who folded their hands on the table and looked up at Greta with pompous adoration in their eyes. Sally sank into her seat. She had personal beef with vice president Lisa Terrace. *Namely, her son called mine a windbag on the playground two years ago, and now they're mortal enemies.* Lisa took it more personally than anyone else. More personally than their sons! "Thank you, thank you! We've got a lot to go over tonight and have quite the full house!"

She could say that again. More people filed in five minutes before seven. They had long run out of chairs. Parents hung out in the doorway and awkwardly bumped into the computers and stacks of books lining the walls. One ambivalent granddad accidentally set off an alarm behind the librarian's desk when his elbow slipped off the counter and bumped into the monitor.

"Order! This meeting is called to order!" Greta smacked a plastic gavel against the table. "Thank you, everyone! Due to so many people being here, let's try to stay on time so we can all get home to our families. First, a reading of last month's minutes..."

Everyone shifted in their seats as they waited for the formalities to end. Most people didn't have the patience for these things, which was why they never came, regardless of how much skin they had in the public school race. This was the countryside, after all. Even with IVF populating half the school district, it wasn't unusual for some families to have up to five children. Two or three was the norm. Sally always heard a joke that said "only children are test tube babies" because their parents were one and done after the financial and biological hassle of IVF. Sally wasn't the only mom with a brood of kids brought to her by a doctor in a lab coat. In fact, the blond woman sitting next to her had five! *It was supposed to be three, but then she had surprise triplets...* Boy, didn't Sally know that feeling.

"...Now we shall address what I'm sure you're all here for." Greta cleared her throat. "As most of you know, in the past few weeks, one of Clark High's own students has been apprehended as one of those responsible for the rash of arsons in our county."

Greta paused. She must have known that sighs and soughs would ripple through the crowd. Murmurs of *"the Musgrave kid"* and *"the one whose cousin is from Alabama"* made their way to Sally's ears. Oh, yeah, everyone knew the story by now. Maybe they didn't know the *whole* story, but they knew enough, and that was all they cared about when it came to saying, *"The Musgrave kid burned all those barns down."*

"Obviously, due to the nature of minors involved, we can't divulge too many details," Greta said. "We can tell you that there is still an ongoing investigation regarding possible other culprits, who may also be minors. It's also possible that they're not from the area."

Greta held off any questions as she read off what the sheriff's department sent her. *I wonder if Candace wrote it...* Honestly, neither Candace nor the others in uniform were great writers or orators, not that they needed to be. Candace knew enough to fill out her reports and submit a weekly log to the newspaper, but when it came to proper statements for the media (and the PTA, apparently,) she often passed some of the buck to civilians. There was a part time assistant at the station. Maybe he was the one who wrote it.

"...If you have *any* leads or information pertinent to this investigation," Greta concluded at the end of her spiel, "please contact Sheriff Albert Peterson or Deputy Candace Greenhill via the non-emergency number. It's in everyone's best interests that we get to the bottom of..."

Finally, someone cracked.

"Lock that little shit up and make him tell you who the others are!"

That started a barrage of comments that required security to look around the room.

"I'm not sending my kid back to school until we know who else is doing this!"

"You ask me, we should round up all the seniors and make them start talking. Don't let them leave the room until they're ratting each other out!"

"Ever heard of the Stanford Prison Experiment? Sounds like we should let the history class have at it or something!"

"Do you know how often my little girl goes to sleep with tears in her eyes? She keeps having nightmares about our house being on fire!"

Greta struggled to regain control of the meeting, her gavel smacking to no end. Finally, a middle-aged man in a black firefighter's dress uniform stood up and bellowed, "Hello, everyone! I am Chief Johnson, from the Paradise Valley Fire Department!"

That worked. Silence befell the library as parents sat down or grumbled against the wall.

The fire chief stood beside the table where the Holy PTA Trinity resided. He left his hat on the end of the table and folded his hands behind his back. "Thank you," he said with his inside voice, which still bounced off the ceiling. "Like I said, I'm Chief Johnson, and I represent the Paradise Valley Fire Department. We are the ones who have been responding to these fires and putting them out before they can spread."

Applause erupted. Sally realized she was the only one not clapping.

"Thank you. I'm here to talk to you, not about the investigation, but what we're doing to ensure the safety of your children in these troubling times. I'm sure most of you have already received notice that there will be special assemblies all this week about fire safety and what to do when you see trouble. Demonstrations will be put on by both members of the PVFD and our local sheriff's department."

A few eyes glanced in Sally's direction. What? Did he think she had anything to do with it? Ha! She was lucky if she found out about Candace doing an assembly before Tucker raced home to talk about it.

Sometimes I feel like I'm the last to know everything. At least she hadn't been the last to find out about the fires. Those were known to the whole town as soon as they happened, and it helped that Sally got out so much. Although "getting out" meant lugging her troublemaking kids.

"I want to stress how seriously we are all taking this," the chief continued. "Not only the fire department, but the sheriff's office as well. Although we cannot provide much information at this time, be sure that everyone's safety is at the forefront of our minds."

"Thoughts and prayers," someone muttered behind Sally. "That's all this is."

Halfway through the meeting, Sally realized that a certain pair of parents were missing. *The Musgraves.* They had never been too involved, but sometimes Sally saw Mrs. Musgrave in the back of the room. Not since her son had been apprehended, however. Last Sally heard from her wife, Dillon Musgrave was under house arrest with a tracking bracelet on his ankle and all electronics ripped from his grasp. She hadn't heard anything about his cousin.

The chief implored people to take some informational flyers about what to do and who to call should they come across pertinent tidbits regarding the investigation. Sally politely declined, since she already knew every number by heart and, well, had direct access to the deputy.

Everyone else knew it too.

"There's Sally Greenhill," she heard somebody say. "That's the deputy's wife. Wonder why she's here? Doesn't she know everything already?"

"I don't know how she can know anything with so many kids. Did you hear what they did at the library last weekend? Totally trashed the place."

"Ha! I saw her at the Crafts & Things the other day, giving Joan Sheffield child rearing advice. Honestly, the last person anyone should take advice from is Sally Greenhill. Do we need more kids like hers running around?"

"I'm telling you, that eldest boy is touched in the head. I see him talking to himself."

"We're going to the twins' birthday party this weekend. Still need to get them a present."

"Get them shock collars."

Sally didn't have the energy to be offended. She heard crap like this and more wherever she went. *Touched in the head? The boy is playing! It's called having an imagination!* Tucker loved to run out into the backyard, drag a stick through the grass, and pretend to go on all sorts of adventures. What was so wrong with that? Sally used to do the same thing when she was his age!

"Hey, Sally."

Chief Johnson stopped her on her way out the door. She returned his cordial greeting. Chief Johnson did not offer her a flyer.

"How's Candace doing? She at home with the kids?"

"Oh, yeah." Sally sighed. "Don't know why I came here tonight. I don't got no answers, and if I did, I'd tell Candy before anyone else."

"She's good people. Has been a huge help in the fire marshal's investigation, I hear."

"Obviously, she doesn't tell me more than she's allowed."

"Of course not. But, ah, make sure you keep an ear out for what the kids are talking about.

Even if they're not involved, they might let slip something they've overheard."

She didn't know why he was telling her this, but Sally thanked him for his concern and rushed out to her car. She wanted to start the engine before anyone had the chance to talk to her.

Chapter 6

CANDACE

"I ain't going back out there," Krys Madison hissed in the backroom of the high school gym, where weights and exercise equipment lay dormant during the autumn months. "Not after that little shit tried to kiss me!"

"It ain't kissing if it's mouth-to-mouth, you know that!" Her partner, a man with the name Quimby stitched into his shirt, jammed his finger into Krys's chest.

"So you go out there and have some pimply sophomore with mega-halitosis lay a big one on you, huh?"

Candace finished going through her handwritten notecards before turning to the firefighters standing behind her. Currently, the high school assembly was dominated by the principal, a guy Candace once knew as the history teacher, Mr. Campbell. *Back then, he was lucky if he wasn't sending half his students to the principal's office.* When the former lunch lady heard that Campbell had gone back to school to get a degree to become the next principal of Clark High School, she had fallen into a fit of laughter. It was either that or cry. Campbell was about as productive as a goose holding up traffic on the highway. *Don't ask me how many times I've responded to those kinds of calls...*

"You two trying to tell me you're afraid of some troublemaking teens?" Candace asked Krys and Quimby. *Like I can't imagine you as a troublemaking teen, Madison.* Krys hadn't moved to Paradise Valley from Portland until well into her twenties, but Candace had a pretty good nose for sniffing out *trouble.* How many times had she almost caught the firefighter driving home with a little too much beer in her system? Candace hadn't arrested her yet, but

Krys knew she skated that fine edge when she had a few drinks. *All sense and reason goes flying out the window with people like her.* Honest answer was to maybe stop drinking after the first two or three or, *heaven forbid,* walk to the bar instead of driving!

Krys huffed when the deputy called her out. "Did you see that little scamp? He tried to lay a wet one on me during the demonstration!"

Yeah, Candace had seen. Had a real good, laugh, too. What did Krys think she got when a sixteen-year-old pock-marked kid with hair shaggier than a dog's waved his hand in the air after a hot woman asked for mouth-to-mouth volunteers? Sure, everyone knew there would be no actual lip-to-lip contact, but Krys couldn't be so professional that she overrode a teen boy's inclination to play a prank.

And say he got to kiss a big ol' womanizing butch like Krys, but that's what life in this town is like. Candace had seen it all as a lunch lady, yeah? She knew what some of these boys, especially those from "traditional" families, said. *"You get three points anytime a girl kisses you. Five points if she's a woman, bro. Ten points if she's gay, and one-hundred points if she's butch! Winner at the end of the year gets to drive the prom limo!"*

The number of boys who had tried kissing her in the cafeteria...

"You know what?" Krys patted Quimby's shoulder. "You go out there and do the next demonstration. I'll hang out here with the deputy and watch the show from the safety of this corner. Next boy will probably try to flash me..."

"Can't do," Candace said. "I mean, I gotta go out there in a bit, as soon as the principal calls me up."

Krys shook her head. "Riiiight. Whatever. I've got texts to return and a mouth to wash out with some soap."

"You want me to scare that boy for you, Madison?"

Krys was already grinning on her way to the bathroom. "I mean, if you're offering."

"...Let's give a special warm welcome to Paradise Valley's very own protector, Deputy

Candace Greenhill." Campbell turned around from his podium and began the applause meant to welcome Candace to the basketball court recently waxed in preparation for the upcoming home game. She took special care to not biff it on her way to the principal. Unlike Quimby, who had slid halfway across the court, much to the great amusement of one hundred teenagers. "Fun fact," Campbell continued. "Deputy Greenhill used to be the lunch lady here when I was the history teacher. We go back, huh?"

Like back then, Candace now towered over Campbell, who cleared his throat and hustled away from the podium as soon as he realized she didn't find him very funny. *Thanks for trying to undermine my authority before I start talking, Aaron.* Oh, yeah, she knew his first name, too. She could really get under his skin if he insisted on giving her some crap.

Nobody clapped as enthusiastically as he did. Probably because this assembly was right before lunch, and the students were antsy enough to slide down the bleachers and crawl out the doors. *At least I'm not on the other side of the crawling, anymore.* The first kid to make it into the cafeteria often heralded an onslaught of famished zombies ready for their lunch of braaaaiiinnnss.

"Thanks, Aaron." Before Campbell had the chance to say anything, Candace wrapped her arm around him and offered a light, friendly noogie. *That* got the audience laughing. *Everyone loves it when you rib on their teacher.* Candace released the principal and took his place at the podium. She tried not to think about how many eyes were on her taser, since she was required to leave her gun behind at the station. *Unless, you know, I'm responding to a call here. Hooray.* That had only happened once. Five years ago, when some clown thought it *cute* to threaten another student with his hunting rifle he was dumb enough to leave in his truck. "Thanks for having me. Now, I know I'm not everyone's favorite person around town," she quickly found Aiden Kitzberg, the boy whose party she had to bust the month before, "but I'd like you to know that I don't hold it against any of you."

A few chuckles rumbled through the gym. The teachers lining the wall shifted between their feet. Oh, Candace recognized them, too. Odds were she'd be saying hello to one quite soon.

"Now, I'm here to talk about something that's gonna make you all roll your eyes, but I'm talking about it because maybe, for once, it will sink in and someone will actually listen to me. Then again, my own kids don't listen to me, so what do I expect?"

More laughter, this time a little louder. Some of these kids were the older siblings of Tucker's buddies and knew him quite well. Namely, they knew what a bossy little bundle of "*Did he really say that?*" he often was.

"I know that people like me and your teachers are always going on about safety and all that." Candace grabbed hold of the mic and walked with it around the podium. Her other hand shot into her pocket. The jingle of her keys – to the cruiser, to her own car, to her house, to the station, to the jail cell – was as familiar as the looks of reverent fear on some of these faces. *Do I like the fact most of these kids fear me in some capacity? Hello, no.* Sheriff Peterson said that a healthy dose of fear was important, especially around authority, but Candace preferred it if the citizens of Paradise Valley saw her as someone trustworthy and reliable, not *scary*. Hell, she'd rather be seen as a bumbling idiot, which was surely what a few thought. "But that's because it's the most important thing we take into consideration when we wake up in the morning and go to work. I guarantee that your teachers are thinking of your safety and your future before they think about grading papers or sending you to detention. You may not believe it, but trust me. I used to have a front-row seat to what teachers in this school thought. Heck, some of them are still here!"

She shot a finger to Mr. Trumball, the PE teacher and JV basketball coach. He shot a finger right back at her.

"Likewise, the first thing I think of when *I* get up in the morning is how I can help protect this town. It ain't about my family... oh, sorry." She directed that apology to Ms. Anita Tichenor, who stood against the wall with her arms crossed. "I'm being a bad influence on your English students."

The laughter got to the point the principal had to ask for students to focus. Candace took that as her cue to concentrate on her message, not on being the approachable, affable deputy any of these kids could come to with their concerns.

"I know it's hard to understand when your priorities are going to school, doing your homework and chores, thinking about college, and whether that pretty girl likes you or not," Candace continued, "but all around you are people who tirelessly think about how to protect you. Because all those things I mentioned? That's your job. You're *supposed* to be self-absorbed and gazing into your own navels. You're kids! But sometimes, we need your help."

She paused for effect. A few kids yawned. Others cocked their heads. The mayor's daughter kept her eyes pointed to the ground.

Poor Christina was still embarrassed about what happened a couple of weeks ago, apparently. *She'll be mortified until the next dumb thing to come her way.* Honestly, making out with Dillon Musgrave had to be pretty dumb, in Candace's humble middle-aged-woman point of view.

"As surely all of you know, a student was recently apprehended as a suspect in an ongoing investigation..."

"Woo, yeah, Dill!" shouted a boy from the top row.

"Cody!" Principal Campbell shouted back.

Candace continued as if nothing happened. "We have reason to believe that he was not acting alone." She did her best to avoid Christina's humiliated gaze. "We know you kids don't actually like telling and snitching on each other, but I want to make something very, *very* clear. If you know anything... if you *see* anything... please do not hesitate to come to me, your teachers, your parents, anyone you trust who can set things in motion. It's not just about arson, either. It's about threats you read on Facebook. Inappropriate messages you get on your phone. If your boyfriend or girlfriend lays the wrong kind of hand on you, someone needs to know. I may be one woman with a badge in this town, but I don't work alone. I simply have some of the best resources to help your hometown."

The mood had changed. Whispers flitted between students. Teachers gazed at one another, as if they didn't know which student to trust. The principal rubbed his palms together, a nervous tic from Candace's lunch lady days. Behind her, the firefighters prepared for the self-defense demonstration that was meant to lighten the mood before lunch. Except Candace knew what had happened.

You don't ask small town kids to turn on one another.

"All right, so who wants to see one of your teachers get put in handcuffs?"

Candace pulled out her handcuffs. The kids hooted and hollered, and the teachers turned away before they were called to the front of the class to be made a mockery of before the students. Candace knew who to call on before she snuck out of the gym.

"How many times has your English teacher said you ain't got no good grammar?"

Convincing Anita to come to the front of the assembly and put on a pair of handcuffs was good, distracting fun, but Candace had bought into her own speech about safety and protocol. How could she convey how important it was for someone to come forward, if they had information? How could she ensure that things in town kept trucking along, before they had the chance to completely fall apart before her?

How could she protect her family? How could she keep her kids from growing up in a world where they feared for their lives?

How could she ease at least *one* burden on her wife's shoulders? Sally already worked her ass off taking care of the house and kids. Every night Candace came home to her wife on the verge of passing out or tearing out her hair. Right now, they had three rowdy kids with a baby about to officially become a toddler. Candace wished they could afford a nanny, even a part-time one. She wished they could afford the only daycare center in town. The only certified one, anyway. She tried not to think about some of the other "babysitting services" there were really under the table daycares.

If Candace could at least keep her wife from fearing for their children's lives when they went out and about, that would be worth it, right?

Unfortunately, cuffing and stuffing the English teacher for the amusement of the school wouldn't guarantee that. Maybe *one* kid would see it and think, *"Maybe it's okay to talk to the deputy, after all."*

She often wondered if her own kids needed that pep talk.

Chapter 7

SALLY

Birthday parties were something Sally *loved*... in the abstract. The planning, the making, and the buying for the party was busy enough, but gave her a dopamine hit that told her she was the best mom in the world. Seriously, how could any other mother compare when she not only bought the *right* kind of Star Wars decorations, but correctly remembered which was R2D2 and who was C3PO?

Yet on the actual day? At the *actual* birthday party? She'd rather die, thanks.

The squealing and screaming of sixteen kindergarteners and some of their other peers tore up the backyard in plastic party hats that soon littered the grass. Sally had thought ahead to cover her dormant flowers and vegetables with protective shells, but the kids quickly tore them out of the ground and flung sharp, pointy ends of wiring and plastic across the yard. The tarp covering the bushes was soon appropriated into a tent for the kids to duck beneath and scream as loudly as they could. The Kool-Aid bowl was overturned as soon as Paige decided it was time for "a little more fun" at the party. The Darth Vader cut-out was made headless by one older boy who shouted, *"Who's your daddy now, Vader?"* The craft table was a big hit, at least, since Sally had set up a place for the kids to make their own paper and cardboard light sabers. Well, it was a hit until they ran out of red coloring, which was apparently the *only* color the kids wanted.

After that, it was time to scream. Again.

Sally envied the other parents who hung behind, taking advantage of the spacious living room and the college football game on TV. The room was evenly split between Ducks and

Beavers fans, both of whom argued with Candace over who had the best quarterback that season. Sally still barely knew the difference between OSU and UofO. Whenever her wife gave her grief, she always said she'd worry about it when Tucker was old enough to think about college.

The parents didn't have to mind their children as long as they were in the living room, drinking lite beer and laughing at the sportscasters getting the state's name so incorrect that all one could do was *laugh*. It helped that people always wanted to be on the deputy's good side. Candace may not have the time to hang out with her old friends on the weekends, but as soon as enough adults were in the house, *everyone* was her best friend.

Meanwhile, Sally rounded up over a dozen children to finish eating their pizzas and get ready for the birthday cake. Her plan was to get the kids to wash up in a basin in the corner of the yard and take a swing at the BB8 pinata hanging from a tree. Well, she *would* have, except Candace hadn't hung up the pinata yet.

Oh, and the bat was still in the garage, alongside the other sports stuff that she had put away... in August. Two months after Sally had asked her to clean a few things up from the yard.

"Mom!" Paige cried, hands gripping Sally's pants as they wandered through a sea of screaming children. "Can we open our presents now!"

"No." Sally shook her daughter off her leg and slid open the back door. "Cake first. You know the drill."

"You let Tucker open his presents early at *his* birthday party!"

How in the world did she remember that? Wasn't Tucker's birthday... wasn't it... *drat, I can't remember when his birthday is.* Sally was either too overwhelmed to think or she was drowning in how old she had become since her first child was born. When *was* his birthday?

"Your brother was well behaved leading up to his birthday, and he asked nicely. *And* I let him open *one* present! That's different from you and Gage opening all of your presents now."

"Mooooooom."

That whine followed Sally into the house. Some school scored a touchdown on TV, and the adults hooted and hollered while flecks of beer spilled onto the couch and high-fives went around the room. Dads beamed with pride that they used to play football. Moms reminiscenced about their days in college. Candace crushed her beer can and tossed it into the recycling.

"Do I hear a birthday girl whining?" she asked the void. Naturally, she received a response from her daughter.

"Mom! Can Gage and I open our presents?"

Sally almost said something, but realized that question was asked to Candace, who held the same title in the house. Usually, they had no problem differentiating which "Mom" the children meant. Context was everything, after all. Yet Sally still thought she was *the* mom at this event. Why wouldn't she be? She had done everything!

"Why, sure!" Candace rubbed the top of her daughter's brown head. "You and your brother go pick one out and let's get started!"

"Candy!" Sally said.

"What?" she shrugged, much to the amusement of the other parents. "Let the kids open one present now. We let Tucker do it as his last party."

Undermined. Sally had been *undermined!*

"Fine." She grabbed the pinata, already filled with Halloween candy, and hauled it outside. Candace followed the twins and their friends to the table of presents. The kids instantly went to the largest one, a gift that had both of their moms' names written on it. *Of course they want the biggest present.* There was a reason Sally didn't want them opening it yet, and it would soon be revealed. She may as well stay out of the mess and hang up the pinata.

"Holy cow!" Gage tore off the largest chunk of wrapping paper while Candace filmed him on her phone. "Look, Paige! It's the Legos!"

Freakin' Legos. They had to go and open the freakin' *Legos.*

"Whoa, whoa." True to his self-appointed form, Tucker held up a hand before his brother and sister could go ripping open the box of

Legos in the middle of the backyard. "Don't do that here. You're gonna lose all the pieces!" Lest Sally assume her oldest was a bastion of sobriety, he continued, "You gotta do it in the living room!"

Thus the box of Star Wars Legos rode high on Paige and Gage's heads as they hauled it into the living room, where the Ducks – or was it the Beavers? – scored again. To the bemusement of several adults, a ton of Legos spilled across the hardwood floors. More children than anyone could handle swarmed the set and started putting everything together.

"See?" Candace said to Sally, who was still tying the pinata to the lowest branch of the tree. "They're distracted now. Concentrate the kiddos into the house so we can clean some stuff up out here and prep for the cake."

"You have all the answers, don'tcha?"

"Hey, hey, I never said..."

"Could you *please* go into the garage and get the bat for this stupid thing?" Sally all but strangled BB8 by his hypothetical throat. "At this rate, I'm taking the first swing."

Candace made herself scarce. Sally did her best to calm down by telling herself it didn't matter what the hell the kids did as long as they were happy. *This is merely a culmination of all your stress. It's not that serious.* Yeah. Sure. Not that serious. She only had half the town watching her as she met a borderline meltdown in the middle of the twins' birthday party.

When Candace returned with the bat, Sally begged her to oversee the pinata. Meanwhile, Sally would clean up the pizza plates, dump some abandoned glasses of Kool-Aid and head back inside for a breather. She needed to sit down at the dining table and remember that this wasn't half as bad as actually giving birth to the little maniacs six years ago. *Forty-eight hours of rolling around a hospital room screaming for someone to sedate me.* Whoever told her the second one fell out right after the first was a dirty, dirty liar. Gage had taken such sweet time following his sister out the birth canal that the doctors fretted in the corner. The only reason they took direct action was because Candace threatened to arrest them for neglect.

"It's okay," she said. "It's gonna be *okay*."

"Having a hard time, Momma?"

Sally looked up from the table to meet some other woman's eyes. *I barely recognize her.* Whose mother was this? Oh, it was Tilly Sandmeyer. Her daughter was around there somewhere.

"Just a little frazzled. Need a break before cake time."

Tilly looked out the kitchen window in time to catch Candace teaching the kids how to swing at the pinata. "At least you've got someone to help you with all the kids."

Is that so? "Candy is a great provider. I'm very grateful for that."

Was that the wrong thing to say? Tilly looked like she had never heard a lesbian say that before. Still, Tilly knew a thing or two about motherhood and how maddening it was. "I'd imagine it's really stressful being the only deputy in town. Even if it's a small town."

"You would be right about that. I don't hold it against her. But... my God, I'm so tired taking care of four kids. The twins alone..."

"I wouldn't wish twins or triplets on anyone!" Tilly laughed so loudly that a few lingering adults looked in her direction. "You're a stronger woman than I am."

Sally grinned. "Thanks. I think I needed to hear that." She didn't mention that when Tucker got into his siblings' shenanigans, she felt like she had triplets on her hands.

"Don't be too hard on your wife, huh? Just the other night she was at my neighbor's house putting the fear of God into him. Guess someone finally called in about those domestic disputes. Or, knowing Deputy Greenhill, she heard it for herself!"

Although Tilly laughed, Sally understood the severity. *Yeah... Candace is always out there breaking up fights and keeping drunk drivers off the road.* She was amazing at her job. Everyone told Sally that she should be proud to have such a hardworking woman for a wife. Didn't she appreciate the money? The benefits? They owned this big, nice house and didn't have to worry too much about healthcare. Hell, the insurance had covered most of her IVF treatments and provided short-term therapy after each of her miscarriages. Wasn't she grateful?

Aren't I grateful?

Sally gazed out the window, where a gaggle of children swung a bat at a big orange pinata. A few adults were in attendance, but Candace was the one showing each kid how to swing a bat for maximum efficiency. Her big smiles were only offset by the matching grins on her twins. They may not be genetically related to Candace, but Sally swore they had inherited her facial expressions.

Yeah, I'm grateful. Nevertheless, Sally was also grateful for giving herself a bit of a break as she settled into her seat and basked in the peace of the kitchen. Until cake time, anyway.

Chapter 8

CANDACE

Sally had been right about one thing. Lately, the twins were so rambunctious that it was like they didn't have an internal off switch. At some point, one would think that they'd wear themselves out and collapse into a pile of snoring kiddos. *Not so much, huh?* Candace wanted to say it was the birthday party that had them so wound up. Maybe that was true, but she couldn't deny that getting them into bed that night was like wrangling cattle. Screaming, hyper cattle.

"I've got a headache." Tucker hopped off the stepstool in the kitchen, a bottle of Aspirin in his hand. "Those butts have worn me down."

"What in the world are you going on about?" Candace snatched the Aspirin out of his hands before he had the chance to swallow. "Children's Tylenol is in the bathroom, if you really have a headache." He was one to talk! Then again, Tucker *had* helped with the baby while Candace corralled the twins in the bathroom and insisted on spraying them down with the detachable showerhead. A proper bath was out of the question, although both Paige and Gage had dirt beneath their fingernails and God-knew-what in their cracks. *Don't let her big smile and curls fool you. Paige is the dirtiest one!* Birth order had something to do with it. Sally liked to say that the twin who blazed the trail out of the womb was the hassle.

That wasn't to say Gage didn't have his moments. Just because he followed a bit more closely than other boys his age, didn't mean he couldn't stir up trouble when nobody was looking. What was that about him getting goop on library books again?

Tucker hopped onto a chair at the dining table. He heaved a heavy sigh, face squishing between his hands. "Tell me again you guys ain't having no more kids."

Chuckling, Candace sat across from him. "Your Mom Sal has made it clear that the shop is closed." For the best. Sally was getting up there in years. Daisy had almost tested Candace's ability to put faith out in the world. Every trip to the doctor's was a nail-biter until that baby was born, and then... "No more kids. Daisy is gonna be the baby until we all die. Which means she'll be the eternally spoiled rotten egg." Paige and Gage would tag-team the crown of Middle Children Syndrome. How *did* that work with twins, anyway?

"Remind me to have a low-key birthday next time, all right?" Tucker hopped off his chair and ambled to a plush chair out in the living room. He grabbed one of his chapter books from the library and sighed his happy way into the depths of the chair.

What in the world is going on with that boy... Candace couldn't help but laugh every time her oldest child acted like he was a seventy-year-old man. Helped that he had the round face and, ah, *rounder* frame to pull it off with success. *He keeps that up, he's gonna be the class-clown through high school.* Unlike the twins, who would win the superlative of, "*Most Likely to Accidentally Set Off a Bomb*" in their yearbook. *I'll have to respond to the theoretical bomb.* Who knows what that would be like in another ten years? Technology moved so quickly...

Candace told her son he needed to get to bed in another hour, but trusted him enough to leave him to his own devices while she wandered into the shower.

What surprised her more? Finding Sally already in the shower, or finding her furiously washing her hair like it was about to fall out?

"Got room for one more?" Candace made sure the bathroom door was locked before taking off her shirt and inspecting her eczema in the mirror. Steam had fogged most of it up, but it wasn't anything a good wipe of her big fingers couldn't fix. "I could really use a wash after today. Think I sweat more in the backyard chasing kids around than I usually do chasing down drunks off the highway." At least once every few weeks she got some rogue idiot who leaped out of his car and gave chase. Usually because he was on his third DUI strike.

Sally said something, but Candace couldn't hear her over the running water and the fan churning overhead.

"What was that, Sal?"

If Sally repeated herself, Candace really couldn't hear.

"Ya hear me, girl?" Candace pulled back part of the shower curtain and beheld the sight of her wife dripping wet beneath the showerhead. Her hair, which had spent most of the day frizzing from the static electricity in the air, was now limp and flat against her back. The only reason people thought Sally was so petite was because, compared to her wife, she *was* a tiny lady. In reality, Sally had some strong, broad shoulders and thighs that meant serious business. She concealed most of her curves beneath sweaters and sundresses, especially after the birth of their first child, but Candace always knew they were there. Outside of the littlest kids who still bathed with Mom, Candace was the only one who got to see the lovely form of her wife's body.

Sally wiped the water off her face and turned around. As soon as she opened her eyes, she shrieked and leaped halfway up the wall.

"Dang, woman!" Candace nearly bumped her head against the shower rod when she pulled back. "Didn't you hear me talking to you?"

"The hell are you doing in here?" Apparently, she still couldn't hear Candace. "You scared me half to death!"

"Aw, come on, baby." Candace stripped down to her birthday suit, leaving a pile of underwear and her jeans on the bathroom floor. "You know I didn't mean to freak you out. Was talking to you the whole time."

"Sorry. I've got a lot on my mind."

Candace closed the shower curtain as soon as she was inside. Only then did she realize that neither of them had turned on the second light in the bathroom. *Ah, that makes this more romantic! Mood lighting!* "I got the twins to bed and Tucker is in the living room reading his book. Last I checked on the baby, she was sound asleep." Candace was damp when she pressed her palm against the wall and cocked her other hand. Wasn't very often she got to put on the charm when she was naked! "So, uh... we got a few minutes to ourselves."

Sally grabbed her hand towel and wiped her face. "Time for *what*? I ain't in a mood."

Apparently. Candace had worked with this before. Sally could often work herself up into a fervor of anxiety and impatience that rivaled the baby's. Usually, all Candace had to do was wrap her arms around her wife's torso and rock her back and forth for a few minutes. People often said that Candace had a healing quality to her touch. That's why the sheriff sent her in to deal with hotheaded suspects who needed to cool down in a jail cell. Okay, so she didn't touch them unless she had to, of course, but her powers often transferred to her stature and her voice. She knew how to turn it on. She also knew how to turn it off when things got serious.

Getting serious was exhausting after a while. When she was home – and the kids were in bed

– she wanted to touch her lady and give her kisses. There weren't many opportunities to be romantic through the week. Not when the baby was crying, the twins were restless, and Tucker undermined their authority in the most passive-aggressive of ways. Sometimes, when the kids cooperated and got their butts to bed in a timely manner, Candace was too exhausted from work and Sally too frustrated that they collapsed into bed.

Candace knew that time was running out for the kind of intimacy they were accustomed to early on in their relationship. *I was starting menopause when Tucker was born.* It wasn't something she often talked about, including to Sally, who was the one who picked up the estrogen prescriptions and made Candace's doctor appointments. Eh, Candace was used to menopause now. She always got hot when sleeping, so what were the hot flashes to her? Her diet could always be better, but at least she stayed fit for work. Nah, she worried more about her sex drive and her mental health. Both of her parents had dementia before eventually passing on in their seventies. Grandma Greenhill stuck around long enough to see the twins be born, but by that time, she barely remembered her own daughter's name.

Who knew how much time she really had left? That's why she made the most of her life now. She spent as much time with the kids as she could, and God knew she made as much love to her wife as He allowed!

...And as much as *she* allowed, since Sally was the Red Light, Green Light in the relationship. So far, tonight was a Red Light.

"I ain't in the mood," Sally said, shooing Candace off her. "Let me finish rinsing off, would ya? Before you go pawing at me..."

"If I were pawin', I'd be grabbing ass and cuppin' tit, now wouldn't I?"

"Oh, yes, you would."

Candace backed off, of course, but she asked to at least have a shot of the detachable showerhead so she could soap up her skin. "Hey, the worst of it is over. I know Halloween is around the corner, but the birthday party was way more stressful. You really knocked it out of the park with that cake, by the way. Was a big hit with all the kids, and didn't taste too bad, either. You think they liked the pinata? Oh, by the way, there are some Legos already popping up in the living room carpet, so..."

"Candy," Sally said, back turned to her wife, "I can't right now. I want some quiet."

Was that a jab at her or not? Candace honestly couldn't tell. *I am a bit of a big mouth...* Once Candace got going, she didn't know how to stop. *Yak, yak, yak, that's me. If I like you.* She liked most people. This was a woman who sat outside the cell on a Saturday night and talked college football with the latest dumbass locked up for starting a fight at the bar. She had her limits, of course. Foulmouthed assholes who took things too far got the silent treatment. People in trouble for serious crimes against human decency got the coldest shoulder that side of Portland. Except that was the rare person in Paradise Valley. Most were decent, once you got past the drink and the anger.

"Tell you what," this was the last thing Candace would say before the end of their shower. "When you're done washing up, go lie down and I'll come give you one of my award-winning massages."

That got a small smile out of Sally. "That is how you got me into bed the first time."

So she remembers? Nope. Candace wouldn't say it. Her wife wanted some quiet, and quiet she would get.

Sally hopped out of the shower soon after. Candace got the whole tub to herself, which meant cranking up the heat and allowing a Tom Jones song to eke out of her throat. Not loud enough for the whole house to hear, of course, but enough for her to enjoy the sound as it bounced off the shower walls. Meanwhile, she thought up a brilliant plan to make her wife feel a little better.

"Sal," she said, walking into the bedroom with only a towel wrapped around her waist. "Hear me out. You, me, the matinee on Tuesday, and dinner wherever you want. You want Dairy Queen ice cream? We'll make it happen. I'll also take you to the nice place out of town. You know, it was good enough for Jalen

Stonehill and that actress of hers, so it's good enough for some clowns like us."

Sally, dressed in a loose nightshirt and with the covers already up around her torso, sighed. "I want to sleep in tomorrow first. Would you mind getting up to take care of the kids' breakfast? I've been running myself ragged and would kill for the extra hour of sleep."

"Tell you what, I'll let Tucker know he can feed himself and the twins whatever cereal they want for breakfast. That way we can both sleep in."

"Tomorrow's Sunday, Candy. They really should have a real breakfast. You know, eggs? Oatmeal? Hell, give them some hash browns and fruit. We've got melon that needs to be used."

"I'm pretty tired, too..."

Candace had no idea what *that* look was about, but she knew it wasn't good. Sally had been giving her that look more and more lately.

"All right." Candace pulled back the covers on her side of the bed and crawled in naked. There were enough afghans on the bed that it made no sense for someone suffering from hot flashes to wear *clothes* to bed. Hell, could they crack the window? Sure, it was dipping into the low 50s at night, but that sounded great to Candace. "I'll get up at seven and make the kids breakfast. I shouldn't be sleeping in too late, anyway. Got my meeting bright and early Monday morning that I need to be fresh for."

"You have nothing going on Wednesday morning?"

"What do you mean?"

Sally turned over, back turned to her wife. "You want to take me out Tuesday night, but aren't worried about being up early Wednesday morning? You know we'll have to find a babysitter too, right?"

"Trust me, I got that part covered. I know who to hassle about it." *Christina Rath kinda owes me right now.* She was also perfect as their occasional babysitter, since she lived two houses down. Girl was a senior in high school. She was old enough to stay up doing some work on a school night, *especially* for the sheriff. Whom had her number now, ahem.

"Uh huh." Sally kicked one leg back, looping it over her wife's shin. "What movie we gonna see, huh? I don't know what's out right now."

"We'll figure it out. The point is to spend some time together without the kids."

"We haven't done that since our anniversary..."

"I know. That's why we gotta do it. Think of it as a chance to wind down after the birthday shenanigans."

Sally was silent for a moment. Then, "Don't you worry that the kids aren't gonna get to see you much as they get older?"

Those words hit Candace right in the heart. "Why, no, I haven't been thinking about that," she said with knitting brows. "Why in the world are you asking about..."

She didn't have the chance to finish her sentence. The bedroom door opened, admitting one young lady dressed in her pink Moana PJs.

"Uh, hello, there." Candace made sure she was properly covered as her daughter ambled over, eyes heavy and hand on her stomach. "Can we help you, young lady?"

"Paige," Sally said with a sigh. "What have we said about knocking before you walk in?"

"My tummy hurts," was all she grumbled, her pathetic visage making Candace's heart fall into her own stomach. *Oh, poor sweet girl. A tummy ache on her birthday?* So what if it was almost over? No kid deserved to be sick or in pain on their birthday!

"You need some medicine?" Candace asked. "Was it something you ate?"

They didn't get a straight answer. Rather hard for a six-year-old to convey her woes when she was too busy throwing up pizza and birthday cake onto the bedroom carpet.

Sally pulled the covers over her head, the sounds of her daughter's retching serenading the couple. "I baked the cake. You clean it up."

The "best" part? Illness and injury with the twins always came in pairs. Candace started the countdown to Gage running in with the same ailment. By the time she saw her son, his sister's face was already over the toilet.

Just another night in Casa de Greenhill, huh!

Chapter 9

SALLY

Coordinating the pickup of her children was an art form. Really. Sally should win the Nobel Prize in physics for constantly bending the space-time continuum to be in two places at once. Because that's what happened a couple of times a week, when she had to be at the elementary school to pick up Tucker at 3:10 and then the library to haul her kindergarteners home from an after-school playgroup.

It had only been thirty-six hours since the Great Throwup of 2019, but once the twins purged the cake from their systems and got a good night's sleep, they were back in business. Not that Sally wanted to deal with pukey kids, but it would've been nice to have them down on their asses for a few days. Besides, she had seen so much vomit and diarrhea in the past eight years that nothing grossed her out anymore. Including those invasive vet shows on Animal Planet. Dr. Pol spent half his days with a forearm up a donkey's ass. Whatever.

Yet that meant the kids went to school on Monday, because Heaven forbid the Paradise Valley-Roundabout school district take Columbus Day off. *Honestly, if the post office and the banks are closed, then school should be closed, too.* At least the library was open as usual. Sally didn't know what she would do if she had to bring the twins home *early.*

She stopped at the elementary school first. The pickup line inched along, right behind the three school buses that served the district. Technically, the Greenhill children rode Bus 12 in the morning, but Sally didn't see the harm in picking them up after school if it meant getting some errands done beforehand.

Since the bank and post office were closed, however, she was ten minutes early picking up her oldest son.

"Now this is what I call *service*." Tucker popped open the passenger side door and hopped inside. They had plenty of time for him to buckle his seatbelt before they had to pull away for the next car, but did he get to it? No. Sally had to give him a death glare before he finally snapped his belt across his chest. On the front steps of the elementary school, two boys from his class waved. "Chris and Dennis don't get this kind of..."

"Don't call it service," Sally said. "Your mother doesn't serve you."

Tucker snapped his mouth closed. "It was a joke," he muttered.

"Don't joke about people serving you." Sally pulled back onto Main Street. Only then did she realize that she had been cruising behind Tilly the whole time. They waved to one another before going their separate ways. "It's not funny. People aren't servants."

"Jeez, okay!"

Sally groaned to see the bouncing kids at the library's main entrance. Of course. They were hers, and they were coming for the backseat at full force.

"Mom! Mom!" Gage flung himself between the two front seats, his breath reeking of chocolate. *Are they feeding my kids sugar again?* When would this insanity end? "Guess what! We got to eat macaroni!"

"He means we used macaroni!" Paige slammed her art project against the back of Sally's headrest. She didn't have to see the dried but gooey macaroni now littering the floor of her car. "Now I want macaroni and cheese for dinner."

Sighing, Sally pulled away again. "We're going to the craft store," she announced. "Your mom needs a break already, and I've got to get some stuff for your Halloween costumes."

"Yayayayaya!"

Those shrieks woke up the baby, who instantly devolved into a tearful fit.

Sally endured it all the way to Crafts & Things, where she was pleasantly surprised to see her friend Joan toiling away on a lazy Monday afternoon. Since nearing the end of her second trimester, Joan had taken her doctor's precautions to heart and spent more time at home. Her partner mostly ran the store on the weekends while friends popped in during the week. For Joan to be there must have meant she hitched a ride with Lorri before she went to work at the hardware store. Did this mean Sally should offer her a ride home? God knew the woman was barely allowed to sit up anymore, let alone walk around too much.

Great. And she decided to bring the brood?

Joan was used to Sally's kids. It was one of the reasons they got along so well. Joan loved kids, and she never seemed to mind the chaotic energy that Sally's kids brought with them wherever they went. Paige and Gage usually lived for the kids' craft corner, but they must have been crafted out after their stint at the library, for they immediately looked at their mother like they needed a nap.

"Can we have the tablet?" they whined at the same time.

Normally, Sally was strict about the amount of screen time her kids got. TV was the hardest to relegate, but when the twins – or Tucker, God forbid – wanted to watch cartoons or play app games on the family Kindle, they could be quite adamant. To the point of rolling on the floor and screaming until Candace barged in and told them to knock it off.

Today, however, she didn't have the patience.

"Fine." She pulled the Kindle Fire out of her bag and handed it to Gage, who had to be reminded to use his indoor voice in the store. They raced to the community craft table and argued over what game to play. Tucker, meanwhile, opened a book in the corner. Five minutes later, he'd be asking to borrow his mom's phone to look something up. That's how it always went when Sally started to cave.

"They sure are wound-up today, huh?" Joan had that look of curious fear. Oh, Sally knew it well. *Same look I had when I was pregnant with Tucker, looking at other moms with their hyperactive kids.* It especially happened in the weekly Wal-Mart runs. Pregnant Sally wandered the baby and children's clothing aisles, watching as one tantrum after another caused a meltdown in that corner of the store. *My future. My God, I knew it.* Tucker had been a rambunctious little baby in her belly, too, always kicking and thumping. Sally knew from the beginning that he would be a willful boy. She lucked out that he was respectful enough.

As they added more kids to the house... woo, boy. Joan was lucky in a way. She and Lorri only planned to have one kid. With any further luck, she'd have a kid like Tucker who, while the occasional handful as all kids were at times, wouldn't give her too much trouble. *Then again, I say this now. For all I know, Tucker will be the worst teenager of my bunch.* Sally couldn't think about that right now. It gave her a headache.

"I swear, they've been injecting caffeine and sugar into their veins every time I'm not looking." Sally popped open her crafting bag, currently propped up in the seat next to hers. "Hoping it's a phase. They were really revved up by their birthday party this past weekend, and now we've got Halloween coming up..." She spread her current project, a costume for Paige, across the crafting table. "Then it starts all over again for Christmas..."

"How's the baby doing?" Joan stuck her face in Daisy's. The baby slept the afternoons away, and after her little tantrum in the car, she was out like a light. Sally gently rocked her in her carrier. A gurgle of compliance made her sigh in relief. "She's getting so big. Do you have any costume plans for her?"

"I got out Paige's old pumpkin costume and will give it a thorough wash soon." In that family, recycling was too important to pass up. Any clothes of Tucker's that weren't totally ruined by the time he outgrew them went straight to his little brother. *Yeah, we're a hand-me-down family.* The only exception were a few shirts that Gage declared, "Really, really ugly!" Those went to the thrift store or the swap meets the American Legion Hall held every few months. "How about you, huh? You know if you're having a girl or boy yet?"

Although Joan's face beamed with excitement, Sally knew she wasn't getting a real answer. "Everything's going great! Minus the endless bedrest. Lorri got me a wheelchair! Can you believe it? I feel like an invalid every time we do our weekly shopping, but then again, I'm only getting bigger every week..."

"Hey, if it means you can get some chores done, so be it. Better to be safe than sorry."

"The doctor is only making me rest so much because of the... well, you know. Anyway, we've decided we don't want to know the sex of the baby until it's born. Gonna love it either way, yeah? We're getting all these tests done so we know how it's doing, so we might as well have one last big surprise when it finally gets here."

"You're stronger than I was. Kept telling Candy we weren't gonna find out, too, but when the doctor offered to tell me, I couldn't help but demand an answer! Besides, my mom was on my ass about what kind of baby stuff to buy me. She's really traditional, you know. She could swing the gay thing after a few years, but was firmly in the blue is for boys and pink is for girls camp. Joke's on her. We've reused all the blue stuff for every baby, boy or girl, since."

"Our nursery is yellow. So it really doesn't matter, was gonna be yellow either way."

"That's how you do it." Sally chuckled. "Screw the whole thing. Pick a color you like. *You're* the one who has to look at it every day! The baby ain't ever gonna remember."

They were not joined by anyone else that day. Joan was grateful for Sally's companionship on an otherwise dreary Monday afternoon. The twins occasionally screeched at something on the tablet, but it was the baby who kicked up the biggest fusses, needing to be changed much earlier than Sally anticipated. When she returned from the bathroom, she found her oldest son hovering by her chair.

"Is it okay if I borrow your phone, Mom?" Tucker asked. "I gotta look up some words."

Sally pulled her phone and charger out of her purse. "You know the rules. No naughty sites, and don't download anything on my phone." She couldn't believe she had to tell him that. In the third grade, no less...

Tucker slammed the charger into an outlet by his chair. Five minutes later, his eyes were glued to the screen instead of his book. *Every time.* With Christmas around the corner, Sally considered getting her son a pocket dictionary to prevent the future screen time.

With the kids as restless as dogs who hadn't been let out all day, Sally could only stay for about an hour. Gave her the chance to catch up on her costume work, but she wasn't anywhere close to finishing. *Don't know when I'm gonna get these costumes finished in time for Halloween.* The kids wore their costumes to school, and that was before she considered the party at the American Legion Hall. Sure, some kids still went trick-or-treating before and after, but the *real* event was the myriad of candy-getting games and costume contests. The school and city hall promoted it to the point that all the kids assumed they were going. *If they don't have a decent costume for the contests...*

Tucker wanted to be Captain America!

"What is that you're looking at?" Sally hadn't meant to snap at her son when she went to collect him to go home. Yet Tucker jerked out of his seat as if she had caught him looking at an adult site. *I swear to God... I'm not ready for that talk yet.* Sounded like something for Candace to do! If nothing else, she knew how to use rural legalese to scare a little fear of God into him!

"Nothin'." Tucker handed the phone back. He had not closed out of the web browser.

Oh, it was nothing serious. On the surface. It was a fansite for one of those video games Tucker liked to play on the family computer. *I can never remember the name. You build things. Little guys come and wreck your things. You build them again.* Tucker often looked up these fansites for tips, tricks, and helpful tools that told him what to do. Harmless stuff, or so his parents had assumed after a perusal a few months ago.

Wait... what is this?

This wasn't just a fansite. It was a chatroom! Oh, hell no.

***

Sally made sure to keep the window open on her phone when they got home. After the twins went into the backyard to play with their new toys and the baby lay down for her nap, Sally sat on her bed, scrolling through the texts her son exchanged with strangers over the internet.

"Yo, did you see the way that thing went up? Literally lit."

"Yeah, man. Saw it on Twitch. Never seen a more satisfying light-up in my life."

"You're only thirteen."

"So?"

Sally scratched her head. What did this mean? What was Twitch? What did they mean by "lighting up?"

"Hey," a new user said further on in the conversation. *"Is there a permalink to it?"*

A link appeared. Sally was almost afraid to click. Yet she did, didn't she?

I don't get it... It was a YouTube link. Yeah, it looked like the game her son played, all the way down to the cartoonish colors and the blocky appearance. But she didn't recall her son's hard work going up in flames every few minutes. Weren't you supposed to stop the fires or discover clever engineering tricks to prevent them from happening? *I really should ask him more questions about that game...* The furthest Sally went with her interest was responding to her son's requests to go over and see what he had built. Candace didn't know much else about it, either. She'd put her hands on her hips and say, "*Well, I'll be. We didn't have this when I was your age. We played Pong...*"

Sally closed out of the video and finished reading the chat.

"*Really sweet light-up, man. I'd love to see that in real life.*"

"*Bruh, not here. You know where to go.*"

Sally closed the browser. For good measure, she ran the antivirus. One never knew what the kids were doing to devices those days.

Chapter 10

CANDACE

Candace kicked herself when she couldn't take Sally out to the matinee that Tuesday night. She was on her way out the station door when a call came in about a suspect fleeing into their county. That meant giving up a whole evening of the two of them. *"I'll make it up to you, promise,"* Candace said before hanging up. *"Even if we have to pay full price."*

The suspect dumped his car on the side of the highway and ran into the woods. Too bad for him, almost everyone chasing him had grown up in the area and knew exactly where to find him. Still, it took three hours, and by the time he was sitting in the Paradise Valley jail cell, Candace's stomach growled for food. *Any food.* She scarfed down the leftover lasagna at home like it was her last meal – then, she promptly collapsed into bed and didn't wake up until her snoring became too much for *her* to bear.

Her chance to take her own wife out on a date didn't come until Friday. At least it made it easier to secure a babysitter for the night. Christina came over with such alacrity that Candace laughed at the spectacle. *Yup. She's still terrified of me.* To be fair, the girl had a lot to fret over those past few weeks. She had matured about five years that year alone, between her mother going out with a new woman and getting swept up in the fiery fury that was burning half of the county. If Candace snapped her fingers and said, *"Get up, girl!"* Christina was already on the other side of the room.

This was fun. Candace wondered how long it would last. After all, teen girls grew out of everything eventually.

"There's leftover meatloaf and mac and cheese in the fridge," Sally said, handing Christina the first half of her babysitting payment. "Twins can stay up until nine tonight. Tucker has to go to bed by nine-thirty. Baby's been extra fussy this week, but I changed her diaper and she might last until we get home."

"Yeah... about the diaper..."

"You've changed her diaper before."

Christina blushed. Was she about to ask for compensation in the event of a dirty diaper? *I would have to admire her chutzpah, honestly.*

"Both of our personal numbers are on the fridge." Sally picked up her purse off the kitchen table and followed Candace to the front door. "We should be back around eleven. Don't care what you do with your phone, but nothing rated higher than PG on the TV while the kids are awake, okay?"

"Yes, ma'am." Christina met them at the door, where she waved them off with the help of the children. "Have a good night."

It wasn't until they were in the car that Sally finally asked, "So, what are we seeing?"

Candace braced her hands against the steering wheel. "Was hoping you had an idea of what we should see."

"Is that new Zombieland movie out yet? I don't remember much about the first one, but it was decent enough. I just don't want to see anything genuinely scary, you know? Ever since I had the babies, I can't take scary things anymore."

Candace started up the car. If nothing else, they could decide what to watch when they reached the small movie theater one town over. *They all start around the same time, so it's not like we're in a hurry for something we don't know we're watching yet.* "Girl, you couldn't handle scary movies *before* the kids came along."

"You're right, but I could at least leap out of my seat without peeing myself. Doesn't work that way after you've given birth three times."

Candace was about to make a diaper joke when she remembered something else. "Oh, but you can watch funny movies? And pee yourself laughing?"

"I was doing that before the kids! I can't help it if I laugh so hard I have to pee."

Which was funny, because Candace was a few years older, but never had these problems. Because it was true. Before Tucker was born, Sally would miss half a standup special because she was trapped in the bathroom preventing accidents.

They had half an hour to kill on their way to the theater. No chance for dinner that night. They'd be lucky to pick something up for themselves in the McDonald's or Taco Bell along the highway. *Going to a McDonald's without kids... can you imagine?* What would they do without the twins begging for toys or Tucker slyly suggesting he get a McFlurry for dinner? The baby cried every time they went to McDonald's. Sally said it was the hum of the lights, but Candace didn't hear anything. Like she didn't hear the baby crying half the time!

What? After a while, you block sounds out, right? Yet she conveniently blamed getting older instead of admitting that, maybe, she was ignoring sounds on purpose.

"You know anything about that game Tucker plays?" Sally asked, somewhere on their trek along the highway.

"The mining one? Or the crafting one?" Like Candace knew. To her, all video games were Mario or Street Fighter. *Oh, the Duck Hunt one was good. I saw they remade it! Too bad it's only for VR. I bet the kids would love to play a game I had in my youth!* She conveniently forgot that it might not quite be the same game as she remembered.

"I think that's the same game," Sally said. "You know me, unless it's Barbie's DreamHouse or Hello Kitty's Island Adventure, I don't know what's going on."

"So what about it?"

"He borrowed my phone the other day to use the dictionary, but – and this is something else we gotta talk about later – I found out he was looking at some gaming site that had a chatroom. They were talking about fires. Did you know you can have fires in that game?"

"Oh, man." Candace sighed, her foot backing off the accelerator as they entered the city limits of the next town over. "Don't get me started about fires right now. I still possibly have a ring of pyromaniacs running around out there getting ready to stir up trouble again. Fire marshal is absolutely useless! Peterson keeps giving me crap about interviewing the Musgrave kid. I think he wants to bring in the FBI. The FBI! You ever hear of a sheriff actually inviting the FBI into their county?"

"I thought most of that rivalry was fabricated by TV. Aren't you always saying you get along with the FBI folk?"

"It depends, all right?"

"Sure."

Candace pulled into the movie theater parking lot. Groups of people shuffled toward the only entrance, where they parted with cold cash to see a second-run film for ten bucks. *Still a better deal than going to a proper movie theater in the city and paying 30 bucks for the two of us.* Candace knew the importance of supporting small business in the area. There used to be a theater in Paradise Valley, way back when such things made more money.

They only showed one movie the whole week, but it usually wasn't a bad one. That's where I took some of my first girlfriends for our dates! Everyone knew the drill. You went to the movie and got pizza for dinner. Most of the people you saw in the theater were the same ones you bumped into at the pizza place later that night. Great way to spread some gossip about who was dating whom!

They picked what looked like the funniest movie, although they had often been wrong before. *As long as we don't see any superhero movies before the kids can...* God, they would never hear the end of it...

Like Candace never heard the end of Sally's ranting about the price of popcorn and drinks. Ironically, Candace was the one who often suggested that they sneak things in. *Not like it's hard... you get deep enough pockets...* Sally also "gladly" paid the fees since she heard on a podcast that the concessions were how the theaters actually made money. *Wish I had time to listen to a podcast every day...* Candace still wasn't entirely sure what they were. It actually took Peterson playing one in the station for her to realize it wasn't talk radio anymore.

Candace didn't realize how tired she was until she sat in one of the back-row seats. Sally plopped down beside her, popcorn and ice in their drinks rattling. Candace relieved her wife of one of the drinks and folded her hand over her stomach. She prayed to God that her radio didn't go off before the end of the movie.

"So, as I was saying," Sally continued, as the previews rolled, "there was something funny about that site Tucker was looking at. We need to have a talk with him about the websites he visits. We've been good at making sure he stays away from adult stuff, but he's getting to an age where he might start chatting with more strangers. I think I'd die if Tucker was lured away from home! We don't know what kind of people are using these sites. Remember that to-do about some of the kids' videos on YouTube? I still get anxiety every time Paige wants to watch one of her princess channels."

Wasn't there a better time to talk about this? Like, maybe, when they weren't in a theater on date night? "You're really diligent about these things, Sal," Candace said. "I'm sure they're fine. Besides, don't go filling my head with stuff about kidnappings and predators. I have to think about it every day already." She still had nightmares from the last time the FBI swept through Paradise Valley. Apparently, a guy was using his mom's basement to upload *very illegal images* to the internet. Candace didn't have to see them for herself to know she wanted to wring the guy's neck. It was bad enough she already had three kids of her own by then.

"Yes, but..."

"Sal." Candace took her wife's hand and squeezed it on the armrest between them. "Tonight's the night for turning that stuff off. We're here to relax and spend some time together, just the two of us. All right?"

Sally grimaced. "I know. I can't help it, though. Something about it is rubbing me the wrong way, and that was days ago."

"I promise to have a talk with Tucker about talking to strangers online." Candace patted her wife's hand. "Promise."

The audience erupted into laughter over one of the previews. Both Candace and Sally half-watched the movie, with only a comment about how the twins would probably like it. After that, they settled into silence, their hands still holding but their attentions elsewhere.

It was what Candace needed after a long month of work. *Surely, it's what Sally needs, too.* She spent so much time with the kids, and Candace knew that they weren't the most well-behaved gremlins in Paradise Valley. *God, I hear about it all the time.* Going to the library, by herself, was a trial. One that featured her on the stand, and head librarian Yi as the starring prosecutor. Oh, Sally did her best, but she was one woman against four hyper kids.

Wish I could afford an au pair, or something. Were nannies available in the area? How much more of a life would her Sally have if there were a nanny to take care of the afternoon goings-on? *I'd give her the moon and stars, too, if I could.* That's how much she loved her wife, who would always fill that role before simply being "the mother of my children."

She wondered how many people thought of Sally as her roles before her true identity.

The movie was passable, but not memorable. They didn't whine about misspending money since, as Candace loved to point out, the point was to spend some quality time together. Dinner was as simple as a walk-up burrito truck that had a mile around the block, but service was so fast that it was like waiting for a restaurant. They ate under the awning until the rains started up again. By then, Candace had finished her burrito and told her wife to finish hers in the car.

Ah, the rain...

It had rained on their first date, so many years ago. *It's Oregon, isn't it? We'd die if it didn't rain for eighty percent of the year.* Yet there had been something special on that long-ago night. Was it the summer sky, covered thought it was? Was it the pretty sundress Sally wore, showing off her toned arms and the shine of her hair? *Maybe it was my cocky attitude that made me excited to be on a date with such a pretty lady.* Sally had never lost any of her luster. She would always be the beautiful young lady who laughed too loudly for most people's tastes. *Where do you think our kids get their boisterous attitudes?* Shocking.

"What are you doing?" Sally clung to the oh-shit handle as Candace made a sudden left turn across the highway. "Is there something wrong?"

What she meant was, "*Some emergency?*" But the only emergency blossoming in Candace's heart had to do with the lack of intimacy they shared in recent months. *Too much going on at work. Too much going on at home. Kids aren't all babies anymore, but they know how to voice their need for attention.* By the time they had an empty nest, they'd be in their seventies. Assuming Daisy actually went off to college when she was eighteen.

Candace parked in front of an overlook into the ravine. A popular picture-taking spot during the day... and a popular make out spot during the night. *Don't ask me how many times I've busted a few dreams here.* Making fun at overlooks was as traditional as rolling around in old barns, but part of Candace's job was making sure nothing silly was afoot. Unfortunately.

Ah, whoever said that she didn't bend the rules for herself at times?

"Remember our first date?" Candace asked. "We talked for hours, looking at this sight."

Rain dripped down the windshield. The car grew a little cooler now that the heater was off. Sally wrapped her jacket tighter to her torso and said, "Candace Greenhill, you did not bring me over here to make out with me like we're two stupid teenagers."

"Aw, drop the mom voice and kiss me." Candace wrapped her arm around Sally's shoulders and laid one on her. The squeals of surprise were exactly what she wanted.

Chapter 11

SALLY

This was a classic Candace move, and so out of left field that Sally didn't know what to do.

Her wife knew the rules. She knew the *law*. No making merry in public! Sitting at an overlook and getting busy was definitely at the top of the county's indecency laws. How many happy couples had Candace interrupted during her tenure in law enforcement? How many bashfully looked away and pretended to not see her when they were in the store? Candace called that the "Glance of shame," as shared by teenagers and grown adults alike.

Yet Sally understood the thrill. They may be no spring chickens, but they were still alive, huh? They had a house full of kids who would never give them a break! Besides, most of them were old enough that Sally became self-conscious that her children not only heard them making love, but understood what was going on. *I would have been mortified as a child. Why would they be any different?*

They couldn't afford a hotel room whenever the moment fancied them. Their schedules didn't sync enough to arrange a weekly excursion for the older children so the adults could have some alone time. With Candace's job being the way it was, there may have been no point, anyway. As soon as the universe heard the stars were aligning for a rare night together, it sent a high-speed chase through the county. Or something like that!

Maybe it wouldn't be so bad to indulge in some harmless fun on their way home...

"See? I knew you got some life still in you."

"Is that supposed to make me feel nice?" Sally grabbed her wife. "You're something else."

"I'm saying..." Candace lowered the armrest and climbed into the backseat. Her struggle to pull her large body through such a small crevice almost tore her pants off. Sally clung to the passenger side door, lest a booted foot came for her face. Yet what Candace lacked in grace she made up for in strength. All it took was one mighty yank, and Sally was pulled into the backseat with her wife. *Ah, look, you can see where the baby made a mess over here...* "It's good to get wild in the backseat."

Sally landed in her wife's lap. With the extra legroom, Candace had no problem opening her thighs wide and creating the perfect little cache for her wife's bottom to fall into, like it belonged there! *How long has it been since I properly sat in her lap?* Let alone like this? Sally wasn't a stranger to perching on the tip of her wife's lap when the living room got a little crowded – although she often had to fight back her own children for the privilege.

"What exactly is your game plan here?" Sally asked. "Because I don't know how much room we got back here, really!"

"Who said anything about a game plan? Don't you know anything about playing by ear?"

"I was never good at music."

"Yet we make such beautiful music together!"

Sally couldn't stand it when Candace got smarmy like that. *She thinks she's soooo suave, using the same old and tired lines I've heard a hundred times before!* Didn't matter if they came from Candace or not. They were tired! And old! Like her!

Aw, maybe not really. She may have been older than Sally, but sometimes it seemed like she had way more spark than the woman squirming out of her wife's lap. *I'm the tired one.*

"Sal," Candace said with a pat to the back. "No frowning in the love machine."

"What if we're caught, huh? What if one of the other deputies or the sheriff find us?"

"Then we get off with a warning! That's how it works!"

"But..."

"You gonna let me kiss you or not?"

She didn't ask if Sally would kiss *her*. That wasn't Candace's style. She started the kissing. She led the nights they spent together. Wasn't that how Sally always liked it? Wasn't that one of the things that attracted her to this woman putting the moves on her?

I mean... I like her attitude, yes... but I'd be lying if I said the biggest attraction wasn't this body. Candace took the stereotypes about cops, especially sheriff's, to heart. She may have been big and stocky, but most of that stock was pure muscle. The kind that came naturally to a select few women who barely had to lift some firewood and, *bam!*, biceps! Their diets weren't as good as they used to be when they were first married, but that hadn't stopped Candace from drinking her protein shakes or getting her exercise. The station didn't have a built-in gym like the firehouse did, but Candace was an avid hiker and tag football player. She participated in the intramurals and bemoaned that Tucker wasn't as into sports... if only because it meant Candace didn't get to volunteer to coach Little League or Youth Soccer.

All to say... she's stacked for her age. Sure, she had a little pudge around the center, and her doctor warned her that certain digestive conditions needed fixing, but Candace was one of the fittest fifty-year-old women in Paradise Valley. Was it any wonder that she had managed the seemingly impossible of becoming a deputy a little later in life?

Was it any wonder that Sally loved to sit in her lap and wrap her arms around those broad, strong shoulders?

"Whatever happened to those cute dresses you used to wear, huh?" Candace futilely searched for a way to get up her wife's skirt. *Kinda hard to do when I ain't got a skirt, huh!* "Remember how easy it used to be to get up to no good in places like the movie theater?"

"We never did that!" Sally would appreciate it if her wife didn't go around spreading rumors like that. *Especially since we came from a movie theater...* "I don't know what you see when you go around tapping on car windows on the weekends..."

"You don't wanna know."

"Right! So why are you putting it in my head when you could be putting other things in *other* places?"

"Next, you're gonna start talking to me about your kegels again."

"When you have four kids, you think about your kegels a lot more than ever before."

"You know what rhymes with that?"

Sally was almost afraid to ask. "What?"

Candace's grin told her that she *should* have been afraid. "Pelvic floor."

How had Sally ended up with such a silly woman for her wife? Did it go both ways? Were they a match made in Heaven? Was it easy to forget everything that frustrated Sally when she was in the arms of her wife like this? Sharing a kiss like this?

Forgetting her woes like *this?*

Sometimes, she wondered how this happened. Maybe not this *moment,* exactly, but certainly this life she had cultivated with Candace. *I can still remember the day we met, but I don't know how we ended up married with four kids.* Like most young women who came to Paradise Valley, Sally had been from a nearby rural Oregon town who decided to find love in the only place built for people like her. Back then, Candace was far from training for her career move into law enforcement. She was barely the head lunch lady at the high school cafeteria. Sally didn't have kids that age now, and she definitely didn't have them back *then*. No, no, they met in the unlikeliest of places...

The bank. We were both standing in line at the bank. Only one window was open on a day when most people got paid. The line stretched out the door. Sally stood in front of Candace, her check from the restaurant she worked at – now closed, unfortunately – pressed against her chest. Candace had become so bored that she struck up a conversation with Sally. Next thing Sally knew, here they were, making out like dumb kids in the back of the family car.

She's hotter now. That's all there is to it.

The wonderful thing about Candace, aside from her drive to provide for her family, was that she always made Sally feel like the sexiest girl in town. That had been true back when they started dating, and that somehow lived to the present day. Sally had been no stranger to physical changes, either. If it wasn't mere aging, it was the four kids and the strain they put on her *after* they were born. Pregnancy? Easy. Childbirth? Over before she knew it. Screaming, the diaper changing, and the errand running that they made her do? That's what made her snore well into the night and feel like a zombie the next day. *It's only going to get harder.* Tucker would be a teenager before she knew it. He'd start his rebellious phase. He'd question his paternity, since it would finally dawn on him that two women didn't make a baby like him. He might resent the younger siblings he was asked to watch. He'd have friends that worried Sally, and girlfriends whose parents drove her nuts. *It hasn't happened yet, and I'm already exhausted.*

But Candace never treated her wife like she was undesirable. If anything, Candace's appetites remained exactly the same. It was Sally who became more tired, more worried, and more convinced that there was no point to making love when the kids were only a shout away. How many times had they been interrupted because a baby started crying or they heard someone sneaking downstairs to the kitchen?

Can't get interrupted here...

Sally kissed her wife so hard that the car started rocking. They both knew what that meant.

***

They found Christina half-asleep on the couch, the TV playing endless *Adventure Time* reruns.

Candace woke up the babysitter while Sally found the rest of Christina's payment. She informed the Greenhills that Gage had put up a bit of a fight about going to bed, but last she checked, he and his sister were both snoozing in their room. Sure enough, when Sally went to peek, she caught Gage with his covers tossed off and his pajamaed-legs hanging over the side of the bed. He had his arm thrown over his face and grumbled when the hallway light entered the twins' room.

"Everybody's asleep, huh?" Candace sat down at the kitchen table, a can of cider in her hand. Only when she approached did Sally realize that another was saved for her. "Does that mean we get a little quiet before going to bed? We're not often up this late..."

Sally took a swig of her cider and said the most brazen thing she had thought of since the back of her car. "We should probably take a shower. Wash up before bed. God only knows what I touched when we were..." she lowered her voice. "*Well,* you know."

"Besides, ain't it my turn to take off clothes?"

"You make it sound like I was naked..."

"Hey," Candace said with a waggle of her eyebrows, "you were naked in *my* mind."

Sally had another drink before returning the can to the fridge. "Why not come up and see all your fantasies come true?"

With any damn luck, their kids would be so fast asleep that they wouldn't *think* about interrupting them.

Chapter 12

CANDACE

The thing that shocked Candace the most Monday morning wasn't finding Sheriff Peterson in the office, when he usually spent every other Monday in another town. Oh, no, what shocked her was the small escort a young man named Dillon Musgrave had. An escort that included his mother and another deputy.

"To what do I owe this great pleasure?" Candace put down her homemade coffee on her desk. There was no reason for this kind of assembly unless she was involved as well. "This looks like a surprise party, and last I checked, my birthday ain't until March."

Peterson rose from his desk, the one unceremoniously pushed up against hers. That desk was blissfully empty for at least half the week. Today, however, it was surrounded by civilians and uniformed personnel alike. "I know this is pretty last minute, Deputy, but one of your greatest wishes is about to come true. Mr. Musgrave is all ours for interrogation."

Candace's mouth dropped. Had this prospect crossed her mind? Sure! Did she think it was gonna actually happen? No! Because someone would have called her that weekend and informed her that an interrogation was on the docket for early Monday morning.

Sorry. It's officially a questioning now.

"Is he offering himself up willingly?"

Mrs. Musgrave butted in on her son's behalf. "As his mother, I want to make it clear that we're here to help clear my son's name of further wrongdoing. Our lawyer will be here shortly. I have it on the sheriff's authority that..."

"Yes, yes, all protocol will be followed," Peterson said. "Young Mr. Musgrave is under no onus to speak until we get into the interview room, and then, it's at his lawyer's discretion. We're... well, why don't you freshen up your coffee, Deputy? We'll have a chat in the other room."

Candace wasn't asked about her weekend. Nor was she allowed any time to get caught up on the minutiae from the weekend. There were too many people filing through the door, from lawyers in business suits to other uniformed officers. It was a mini reunion for the county sheriff's department, but Candace didn't get to shoot the breeze over coffee or ask some questions that had been burning in her ever since she filed the last weekly police report with the city newspaper. Everyone was there for one reason, and as soon as business was concluded, they were heading back out to their posts again.

One of the lawyers was the county DA from the seat. He had a private conversation with Peterson before motioning for Candace to join him in the other room.

Nothing was out of the ordinary. A refresher about what was and wasn't legally allowed with a minor, as well as any deals that might be on the table. Unsurprisingly, the DA was prepared to charge Dillon Musgrave as a minor and reduce his charges if he turned over any useful information about his supposed accomplices. That was the whole reason they were here. Dillon still thought he had something worth hiding, but as soon as his mother heard that deal, she dragged him in by the scuff of his neck.

Candace cracked her knuckles and announced she would be ready as soon as she grabbed some more coffee and prepared the recording equipment. She still wasn't the best at figuring out the tech, but at least she wasn't Peterson, who once blew out a wall socket finagling with a device.

Their only interview room felt much smaller with four people in there. It would have been five, but Peterson cited mild claustrophobia as his excuse for joining the DA on the other side of the window. It was Candace vs. Dillon and his guardians, which included his mother and the attorney the deputy had never met before. He must have been from the city – which meant he not only knew a few laws, but was prepared to charge for his knowledge.

Since the Musgraves were undoubtedly being charged by the hour for this privilege, Candace would do them a favor and get going.

"How ya doin', Dillon?" She leaned back in her seat, pen thumping against her legal pad. The notes were for her own benefit, in case she was called back to testify later. The AV equipment would do well enough recording the exchange. "Bet you're enjoying all this time off from school. How long has it been, huh? Almost a month since you've been under house arrest?"

"He's no truant," Mrs. Musgrave said. "We have him doing alternative education over the internet to keep him on track to graduate. Supervised, of course. It was arranged through the DA's office."

Candace didn't give a flying crap if Dillon were suddenly a new Einstein with his home studies or had spent every day of his house arrest staring at his ceiling. "I'd prefer to hear what he's been up to from his own mouth, if you don't mind, Mrs. Musgrave."

Dillon, who kept his chin pointed toward the table and his eyes downcast into his lap, slightly turned his head to the side and snorted. "Nothing. Hanging out and reading, when my mom's not making me do math sheets."

"Must be real lonely having all your electronics taken away from you, huh? Can't talk to any of your friends from school... or online."

"They're all punks, anyway."

"Dillon," the attorney said. "Remember what I said about the language you use?" He looked to Candace and said, "What my client means to say is that his friends have not been forthcoming with wanting to visit."

"He's not allowed visitors, anyway," Mrs. Musgrave cut in. "He's grounded on top of being under house arrest. No friends."

"They ain't coming around, anyway."

"You've got your cousin to talk to, right?" Candace asked.

"Who? Carrie? Are you kidding me? I'd rather talk to the dirt on my shoe! She's a nark!"

Candace chuckled. "I'd nark on you too if you lit the barn I was in on fire."

"I told you all, I had no idea anybody was in there!"

Dillon was halfway across the table, hand slapping against metal and spit flying toward Candace's face. She didn't flinch. *I'm not afraid of no kid. Especially no kid with his mom right behind him.* Never mind the sheriff behind Candace.

Even so, the family attorney pulled him back into his seat and whispered something to both him and his mother. Mrs. Musgrave nudged her son, who muttered an apology.

"I know the events, don't you worry. Besides, your cousin Carrie corroborates that you probably didn't know that she and Leigh-Ann Hardy were in that barn when you lit it up with Christina Rath."

"Told you, Christina didn't do nothin'."

The lawyer interrupted. "My client merely wished to show off for his new girlfriend. We've already cleared Ms. Rath's name, so let's carry on."

"Right. I'm not really interested in Christina," Candace said with a lackadaisical shrug. "I'm interested in your other friends. Maybe your online friends. The ones you say have a vested interest in making things go up in smoke around here. So far, you've been reaaaallly quiet about any of your firebug buddies. Now, you can't go dangling that juicy information in front of our faces and then snatch it away. Really good way for you to make some of your friends in the sheriff's office none too happy and willing to help you. The whole reason we're here is because we have come to an agreement, from what I understand."

The lawyer lowered his head toward Dillon's again. "Remember, the whole deal falls through if you don't give them something they can work with. It's not about being a nark, Dillon. This is way more serious than what any of those people can do to you."

He shared a look with Candace before sitting up. "Best listen to your lawyer," she said.

"What's got you so scared about turning them over, anyway? Are they in a gang?"

"No," Dillon muttered.

"Have they threatened you?"

He was silent.

"All right, how about this?" Candace leaned back in her seat, the chair creaking with every heavy movement. "Have you ever met any of them in real life? Or only over the internet?"

After more prodding from his mother, Dillon finally said, "I've never met anyone else into it in real life. They're careful about that."

"Yet you say you're only responsible for a couple of the fires, not all of them. That tells me they've been around town. How do you know they take credit for them, if you've never met them or weren't there?"

"'Cause they said so online."

"Did they provide any evidence, such as pictures or videos?"

"Yeah..."

The lawyer motioned for Mrs. Musgrave to hand him something. With a small jerk of her shoulders, she reached into her purse and pulled out a small smartphone with a black and neon green case. It had Dillon's name all over it.

"Here is one of the videos we've already sent the DA's office," the Musgraves' attorney said. The phone was soon in front of Candace's face. She pressed play on a video. Sure enough, it was one of the first barn fires of that past summer season.

The DA tapped on the window. He motioned that the video wasn't worth Candace's time.

"Right. Thank you for this." She placed it face down on the table and refocused her attentions on Dillon. "If what you say is true, it shouldn't be too hard for you to give us some information to identify the other culprits."

At first, she wasn't sure he was going to say anything. His line of sight made a sharp turn from Candace's face to the far corner of the room. The only sound was the hum of the air conditioner as it churned air back into their faces. The phone remained overturned on the table, taunting Candace with promises that she could identify somebody's voice, which had already been torn apart by county forensics.

"You're never gonna catch 'em all," Dillon said with a deep, disgusted voice. "The network's too big, all right? There are hundreds of people in the group in this state alone. I don't know how many more in Washington. Maybe they got some in California, too. What, you want me to rat them all out? You want me to put that kind of target on my back? Today, it's some abandoned barn nobody cares about. Tomorrow, it's my house."

Mrs. Musgrave gasped. "I don't know anything about this," she insisted.

"That's the whole thing about a surprise retaliatory attack, Mom," Dillon said with a snort. "You're not supposed to know anything!"

"Where is this network?" Candace asked. "Is it online? Some kind of group? Forum? Facebook?"

"Forums? *Facebook?*" Dillon was nearly in stitches by the time he got his act back together. "How old are you, anyway? Nobody goes on those anymore!"

Candace folded her hands over her legal pad and leveled her gaze on the boy acting the tough sport in front of her. "Dillon," she said, "this is it. This is your chance to avoid the kind of crippling, criminal punishment that could affect the rest of your known life. If you want a chance at *any* kind of future, you'll help us figure out who is terrorizing our town. You're already going down for some of the fires. The least you could do is bring the others down with you."

He was silent again, studying the lines crossing Candace's aging face. *Youths always love to remember how young they are. They act like they're not gonna be sitting here in my spot in another few years.* Those years would go by so quickly that they wouldn't know what happened. Nobody did.

Finally, Dillon spoke.

"They're everywhere," he said. "Take a look outside, and you'll count the number of kids getting off on this stuff."

If his goal was to unsettle her... well, she hated to admit it, but for the briefest second...

She was a bit unsettled.

Chapter 13

SALLY

Tucker waited until the last minute to tell his mother what he wanted to be for Halloween. When the words *"vampire police officer"* came out of his mouth, Sally tilted her head, as if expecting him to follow that up with an explanation.

The boy was in third grade. What other explanation was necessary?

She knew where his desire to be a police officer came from. This was a boy who looked up to Candace with awe on his face. Like most boys his age (and younger,) Tucker was fascinated with uniformed personnel, from the police down at his other mother's station, to the firefighters taking out a blaze two blocks away. On Veteran's day, a few of the old combat vets got out their uniforms and held meetings down at the American Legion Hall before going to get a late lunch at Heaven's Café. Tucker was always the first one with his face pressed against the glass and asking the vets questions about their uniforms and what it was like being in the Navy. Or the Army. Were there any Marines in the house?

The thing that confused him the most wasn't how Candace became a deputy when he was still a baby. No, what confused Tucker Greenhill more than anything was how Candace *wasn't* a vet, too. Most of the other law enforcement officers had stints in the Army and Air Force. How did Candace claim her "combat" experiences in "high school lunchrooms?"

Sally had the answers to that, but her son was too young to understand the complexities of military culture and old policies that made Candace think twice about enlisting when she was younger. *One of the things that inspired her to finally switch careers was the shift in public thinking ten years ago.* It was amazing how much had changed in a decade. Sally and Candace used to agree that they would probably see legalized gay marriage before they died, but that was still decades away. The thought that they could be legally married in Oregon, one of the first states to ban it in their constitution, blew Sally's mind.

Everything changed like a domino falling at the start of a line. Back when Candace looked at her bride and said, *"I'm seriously thinking about quitting my job at the high school and going into the police academy..."* Sally had feared not only for Candace's safety, but that she would be laughed out because of her age. What she hadn't anticipated was how determined one woman with a love for working out could be. Then again, she had married a woman determined to have four kids before menopause!

The money for IVF and hospital stays hadn't been possible without the good insurance

Candace got with her new job. Their affording a house big enough to house their growing family hadn't been possible without it. Sally becoming a stay-at-home mom who didn't need to pick up a part-time job while the babies were young hadn't been possible until Candace stepped up and followed her dreams.

She was someone worth admiring. Hearing that Tucker respected that and wanted to dress up for Halloween was worth the extra work it might take. But... the vampire part...

He didn't merely want fake fangs and some pale makeup for Halloween. He wanted a costume that reflected his role as "the underground's #1 cop!"

All right...

They lucked out and found a basic children's police uniform at one of the seasonal Halloween stores. It came with a plastic hat and pair of fake handcuffs that were easy enough to distress with red paint made to look like flecks of blood. They tossed aside the badge and made a new one out of paper mache, so they could write whatever role Tucker wanted to portray.

Whatever makes him happy. Sally was already in plenty of trouble with the twins' costumes. Anything that made Tucker's easier was a win in her book.

She stayed up late the Sunday before Halloween, doing last minute alterations to Tucker's costume. Her son was the only other family member still up at nine, although she was to shoo him off to bed as soon as she had him try on the shirt again. For now, he hung out in the living room, playing an old video game on the TV. Sally's only request was that he keep the volume down so everyone could sleep.

Somewhere between checking up on him at nine and popping back out at 9:15, she realized he had swapped over to that pixelated building game that continued to flummox both of his parents. *It's one thing for me to admit I'm older and don't understand what kids are doing these days... but I really do not understand this.* What was the goal? The end game? How did one "beat" it? Candace had tried explaining to her wife that it was like The Sims, but Sally never understood that game, either. Not even when a friend showed her what happened when one took the ladders out of the pool.

Tucker's favorite game reminded his mother that they were supposed to have a talk about internet safety. Because Sally was pretty sure that her wife hadn't done it, since Candace was beyond busy with the Musgrave boy and his half-admissions about who helped him set those fires. Every night they went to bed, Candace said, *"Tomorrow, I'm getting some real answers."* Every evening, she returned home from the station saying, *"Tomorrow..."*

Candace was in bed now. So were the twins, and the baby hadn't kicked up a fuss in a while – so, she was probably due. Sally looked between the back of her oldest son's head and the project in her hands. When she finished a stitch to make the sleeves a little tighter around Tucker's elbow, she said, "When you've got a moment, Tuck, I need you to come try this on."

He whipped his head over his shoulder and leaped up as soon as he realized his mother hadn't urged him to go to bed. Before Sally could sit back down at the dining room table, her son was in the chair next to hers.

"What do you think?" Sally showed him the red stitches she added to make it look like blood came out of his front pocket. "Kinda afraid we're going more zombie than vampire. You sure this is what you want?"

"Whoa, that's cool!" Tucker snatched the top out of his mom's hands and held it up to the chandelier light.

There were still a few alterations to make, as evident when Tucker futilely tried it on a few minutes later. Sally jotted down some notes on a scrap piece of paper and realized she would be up at least another hour to make the changes. Oh, well. She had slept in that morning. She could afford to lose a little sleep on Sunday mornings.

"Hey, have a seat." She patted the chair Tucker had leaped from like a frog attempting to return to his pond. "We've got something to talk about."

She tried to say it with a sliver of good humor, a reassurance that Tucker wasn't in trouble. Yet her son looked at her as if he should have run out the back door instead of sitting back down. "Yeah?" he asked. "Whatever Paige and Gage said I did, I didn't."

"They haven't said anything. Should they have?"

"This is *entrapment,* Mom."

"How do you know a word like that?"

"From Mom."

"You need to stop watching *Law & Order* with her." Candace claimed it was a bonding moment for her and Tucker to watch select police procedurals, but Sally feared her son wasn't yet old enough to handle the mature themes. This was a boy who still had nightmares from those *X-Files* reruns he saw in first grade. "No, we need to talk about something else. It has nothing to do with what you've done. It's more like... you're old enough now to hear some things."

"If this is about sex, I already know about that."

Sally dropped her pen and piece of paper. "Excuse me?" She did not recall discussing *sex* with any of her children! Where was he hearing this? From Candace? Yeah, right. Even if she got it in her head to tell their oldest about the birds and the bees, how did she find the time? "How, pray tell, do you know about *that?*"

He shrugged. *"Law & Order."*

Yeah. All right. Sally wasn't digging into that, but she made a note to talk to Candace about what their son was exposed to on TV. *There's a reason they have to watch PG content with a babysitter!* Sally always stayed on top of what they were watching on TV and YouTube. Preferably, to prevent this awkwardness whenever possible.

"This isn't about... that." Sally picked up her phone, which was already down to 10%. *Damnit. Hold out on me, phone.* She unlocked the screen and brought up the browser tab she never exited. "I want to talk about the kind of people you might talk to on the internet."

Tucker shifted in his seat. That wasn't guilt on his face as much as it was dread. *No matter what, he thinks he's in trouble.* When a boy thought he was in trouble with his mom, things could go one of two ways. Either he would blab about whatever she wanted to know, or he would clam up. With Tucker, there was no way to tell which way this would go.

"You know I don't have a problem with you looking up stuff about your games. Why, in my day, we didn't have..." Sally cleared her throat. "I mean, it's quite extraordinary what you kids have access to these days. This whole internet thing is pretty new. I know you've had it your whole life, but your moms didn't have internet in the house until a couple years before you were born." Paradise Valley hadn't been hip with fiber until 2008, and that was only because a major telecommunications company ran wires between Portland and the coast, anyway. "But that means you're getting to do things I don't know much about, and I want you to explain something to your old, dumb mom."

Tucker perked up again. Oh, good. He thought this was his chance to be a know-it-all.

"You left this window up the last time you used my phone. Remember, in the craft shop? Anyway, I was wondering how it was you got to talk to other people. Do you know who these users are? Are they from school? How would you find people like that to talk to on a website?"

Tucker stared at the chatroom, left static since the old conversation a couple weeks ago. When he spoke, it was with the tone of a boy who knew he had to tread carefully. "I don't have an account for that, Mom," he said. "I found it when I was looking something up. See, sometimes your stuff catches on fire, and you have to figure out how to keep it from spreading and ruining all your progress. But I guess some people make it happen on purpose because they think it's cool."

"So you don't know who these people are?" Sally faked a sigh. "Too bad. I was hoping I could find some crafty people to talk to."

"No, I don't know them. They're from all over the world, I guess. Although..."

"Hm?"

Tucker sucked in his cheeks and chewed on his bottom lip. The boy had answers, huh? What was keeping him from sharing anything?

He knew he wasn't in trouble, right? Or had something bad happened in one of these chat rooms? Sally knew that the boogeyman of some pervert luring her son away from home was so unlikely that she was better off worrying about car crashes, but wasn't it *strange* how he acted like he had said something he shouldn't have?

"There are kids at school," Tucker began, "who use chatrooms like that to meet people. You can actually set your location so you get people in your area. I say they're from around the world, but if you have your location available to the website, they match you up with people in your town, I guess."

"Wow. You know all that, huh?" It never ceased to amaze Sally how smart kids were these days. Seemed like the more computers they grew up with, the more likely they were to learn rocket science before fifth grade! "That's amazing. So you can actually find some kids from this town talking about topics from visiting a few websites?"

"Oh, yeah. Not just kids from here. It's mostly Portland kids because it's the big town.

Everyone uses usernames, though. I don't know who they are, honest."

"Interesting. You know not to talk to strangers, right? Not without making sure you keep all your personal information..."

"Yeah, yeah." Rolling his eyes, Tucker hopped off his chair. "Don't talk to strangers. Don't use my real name. Don't tell anyone where I live or go to school, or who my parents are. They tell us all this stuff at school."

"That's good." Sally watched after her son as he marched back to the living room. "Make sure you wrap the game up in ten minutes, Tuck. You've got school in the morning."

He still put up a fuss ten minutes later. Apparently, something in his game had caught fire, and he couldn't shut it down until it was finished ruining his hard work.

Sally felt for him. Really. He still needed to go to bed.

After ensuring the game was shut down and her son was in his room, Sally returned to the dining table and opened her phone, which only had 6% battery left.

"PV has the best kindling." That was a message Sally conjured when she scrolled back up through the conversation. She felt like there was something here. Something she could show her wife and say, *"See! Go get* these *kids!"* Yet her inability to make sense of her own phone most days made her bite her tongue and resign herself to more research – when she had time. God, she never had the time.

Chapter 14

CANDACE

Didn't matter if Halloween fell on a Monday or a Friday. The first day of that week heralded the return of smartass shits who thought it funny to egg and TP houses between Paradise Valley and Roundabout.

Did Candace have something better to do with her precious time? Of course! Yet she was the one radioed to respond to non-emergency calls about eggs on an old man's porch and a bag of dog crap that refused to stay alit.

...Yet the old man still stepped all over it.

"I'm telling you, I've had enough of all these destructive urchins!" Mr. Graham wagged a wrinkled finger in Candace's face as she took his statement and tried not to roll her eyes. The crisp autumn air grew colder with the passing days, and all she wore beneath her jacket was a short-sleeved shirt and her bra. *Suppose I should put on my bullet-proof vest for these fine occasions.* Would they protect her from an ovular projectile? "When they're not out there lighting everything on fire, they're egging my house!"

Candace would go out on a limb and say they weren't the *same* kids, but she also wouldn't say that in front of Mr. Graham, who was on a tear. Besides, her job was to show up, take a statement, and assure him that they would keep looking into it. Should the culprits be found, she'd give them the sternest talking to and highly suggest that they drop by Mr. Graham's place and help him clean up.

"It was that Doolittle kid," Mr. Graham insisted. "The one with the red curly hair and the pants down by his ankles."

"You mean Chester Doolittle?" Candace laughed, flipping her notepad closed. "Why, he graduated and moved away a few years ago. Last I heard, he was in California."

"California! They're the ones sending their kids up here to make a mess of everything! Did you know my new neighbors are Californian? They tore up that nice forested property, laid down the foundation for some *summer home,* and then left it! Packed up their tools and left the foundation to rot in the rain. How many Californians are gonna keep doing that, huh? We don't have unlimited resources for them to come in and..."

Candace checked out after that. *The only rants I hear more than "these darn kids" are "those damn Californians."* As a born and bred Oregonian, Candace had heard those rants forward and backward for half her life. Sally had heard them, too, since she came from one of the trendier – yet poorer – areas of the coast, where before the housing crash, Californians (and Arizonans, and Texans...) bought up tracts of land for residential development, only to leave everything barren and half-finished after losing everything in 2008. Some wounds never healed with the locals. Especially when the half-finished development jacked up property taxes.

"Who's gonna help me clean this up, huh?" Mr. Graham followed Candace. "You gotta find those kids and make them clean it up!"

That was the last thing she heard before saying farewell and driving to her favorite end-of-the-month speed trap spot. While the location never changed, the day of the week did. *I remember, before social media, it was a lot easier to surprise the locals with speeding tickets.* Now, however, *she* also received group texts along the line of, *"Saw Greenhill behind the mileage sign by the Pump 'n' Go! Watch out!"* She only had about an hour to keep any element of surprise once she parked, speed gun out and a bottle of La Croix attached to her hand.

She'd get something good. At this time of day, after school got out? She always did.

She didn't expect to have someone speed by so soon, though. That was like Christmas coming early, since Candace enjoyed nothing more than firing up her siren and pulling out onto the highway like she had lived her whole life for this moment. It wasn't that she wanted to *scare* the people in the old 2002 Ford Taurus, but she bet they had a nice and good *oh shit* moment when they saw the lights and heard the sirens bidding them to pull over. Now.

They weren't in any hurry to pull over, though. One head turned around and looked through the back windshield. In a crazed fashion that suggested either drugs or guns, two kids in the backseat scurried to hide items Candace was probably *very* interested in. Because why wouldn't she be? If they were interested enough to hide it, she was interested enough to find it!

Eventually, the car pulled onto the shoulder. Candace double-checked her dashcam before getting out of the cruiser and slowly approaching the Ford Taurus.

Three... no, four teenagers. All boys. Their dark hoodies were the norm for the area, but not the nice, torn jeans that looked like they could house a circus. Well, one boy had jeans so tight that Candace was half-concerned for his private parts. *Don't they gotta breathe?* Whether the pants were huge or tight, however, didn't matter. What mattered was how guilty they looked.

Candace didn't see anything damning, though. No spray paint bottles. No alcohol. Not a carton of cigarettes or a vape pen. Just a lot of empty junk food packages.

"Good afternoon." She put her hands on her hips, thankful that the driver kept his hands at ten and two. At least they were still teaching *that* in driver's ed. "Have any idea how fast you were going back there, young man?"

The kid in a black hoodie and with a plethora of pimples on his face couldn't have been older than seventeen. Maybe sixteen. Old enough for a license, not old enough to be carting around a ton of friends who were probably more distracting than texting on his phone. *Come to think of it, none of them have their phones out. Interesting.*

"No idea, officer," the driver said.

"Do you know the speed limit on this stretch of highway?"

"Um..." He barely glanced at her. "Fifty-five?"

"That's right! Now, how fast do you think you were going?"

"Fifty-five?"

"Try sixty-five." Candace chuckled. "Where are you going in such a hurry? You and your friends got some video games to play? None of them look to be in labor."

One of the kids in the backseat laughed. Candace shot him a look. He shut up.

"Sorry. I... I didn't..."

"License and registration please, young man."

All of this was routine, thank God. Candace had to wait thirty seconds for the teenaged boy to root around his glove compartment for his registration. His license was freshly printed at the nearest DMV. *Roundabout, huh? He must go to Clark High. So why don't I know him?* There was no way all four boys were so unknown to her. Even if they had moved there at the start of the new school year, she would have met them by now. *I make a point of memorizing most of the kids I see come through here, after all.*

"Where are you boys all from?" she asked, as if making small talk.

"Roundabout," the driver said.

"Your friends?"

They all said a different place. The chuckler in the backseat was from Hillsboro. The passenger side guy was from Tigard. The super silent one in the back was from Cottage Grove. *Quite the disparate group of young men, if you ask me.* The only thing they had in common was their age bracket. Legally, she was only interested in the driver who had been speeding for no reason beyond, *"Guess I didn't notice."* That earned him a firm warning. Had they been mouthy or disrespectful – or, God forbid, lied – she would have written him up. Yet since his record showed no other infractions yet, she let him go. She might be seeing him around, anyway.

As for the other boys... if they really were from where they said they were, then Candace was intrigued. She couldn't put her finger on *why* she cared, though. Was it the feeling in the air? The threat of mischief? Or was it the fear of something bad happening, although at least one arsonist was caught already?

"They're everywhere," Dillon had said. *"Take a look outside, and you'll count the number of kids getting off on this stuff."*

That was the soundbite playing in Candace's head every time she saw a group of young men – or women – that she didn't recognize. What had they been hiding in the backseat before they pulled over? Candace should have asked more questions. A part of her also considered that there were four of them and one of her. Perhaps she was stronger than all four of them combined, but did she want to take her chances?

She sat in her cruiser after letting the boys go. A part of her hoped she wouldn't come to regret it.

Chapter 15

SALLY

If Sally thought the twins' birthday was a living madhouse, she had no idea what was in store that Halloween.

The most important thing? Getting the kids off to school. In costume.

"Raise your hand if you haven't forgotten your hat." She had donned a witch's hat for the occasion of driving to school. Tucker, however, had sauntered to the front door with his backpack and coat, but had conveniently forgotten the one thing that would keep his head warm that day. "Not so fast, Tuck."

"Ah, darnit!" He raced back upstairs while the twins danced around their mother's feet.

"I'm gonna get so much candy at school!" Gage tossed his Captain America shield into the air, while his sister played with her homemade Wonder Woman tiara. She wasn't allowed to take the magic lasso (also homemade) to school, however. Something about it being a very dangerous weapon. The good news was that kids that age couldn't care less, so off she went into the car with barely a jacket and shoes on her feet. Sally chased after her, and Gage continued to prattle about toys and candy.

The one thing Sally was thankful for? She didn't have to take them out trick or treating that night. She would be in a different kind of hell as soon as the party began at the American Legion Hall, but at least it was *contained* hell!

Tucker was the last to throw himself into the car. Sally pulled into traffic and immediately regretted the hat slipping down her face.

No rest for the weary. That's what she glibly told everyone she bumped into after dropping the kids off at the elementary school. She rushed to the supermarket and picked up the candy now on clearance. *Never know if we might get trick or treaters!* Nobody would be home, but the least Sally could do was leave out a bowl of candy for whatever enterprising child came by with a bucket or a bag. *Or the teenagers will ransack it. It's the spirit of Halloween!*

She already foresaw some issues with the twins' costumes and turned back to the craft shop. Joan wasn't in that day. Instead, she bumped into two of the least likely people helping the crafty owner keep her store open while she was on bedrest.

"Don't put those up there!" Abby Marcott jabbed her cane against her granddaughter's legs. Unfortunately for Mik, she was halfway up a ladder, and a jab to the legs meant she almost went down. "Are you daft? They go in *reverse* rainbow order! You start with violet, not red!"

Mikaiya apologized as she scurried down the ladder and offered to get Sally whatever she needed. As soon as she found it. Somewhere. Around the shop...

The bank lines were the most ridiculous, and Sally had forgotten about their strict no hat rules. One of the tellers laughed to see the lopsided witch's hat on top of Sally's head, but another not-so-nicely asked her to *please* take it back out to her car.

The only moment of reprieve she had that busy Thursday was when she dropped by the police station. Candace was far from drumming her fingers against her desk. She only had time to confirm with her wife that she would, in fact, call her if she would be out late that night. "Aren't I always out late on Halloween?" Candace asked with a shake of her head. "Even if I don't get any calls, I have to park outside the bars and wait for some drunk idiot to get into their car. Every year like clockwork."

"If it's getting close to ten, I want to know if you're gonna be home or not." Sally adjusted the hat on her head. "Now, if you excuse me, I have to go pick up the twins from kindergarten. I'm expecting a full knock-down Marvel fight in the schoolyard with how many Iron Men and Aquamen I saw filing into that school."

"Aquaman? Thought he was DC?"

"You know I have no clue." Sally gave her wife a kiss on the cheek and took her leave of the station. "Good luck, hon. Be safe tonight!"

"That goes double for you! You've got all my babies!"

Your babies, huh? Sally slipped into the driver's seat of her car and started the engine. *Never mind they all leaped out of my womb. That's right. Leaped!*

Before she released the brake, she picked up her phone and checked her notifications.

There was a voicemail from the school.

"Hello? Mrs. Greenhill?" That had to be the secretary. Sally would recognize that snooty voice from anywhere. *Only a woman who has worked around kids her whole life yet never had any of her own can sound this snooty!* "So sorry to bother you, but I'm afraid Tucker isn't feeling too well. Could you drop by? We currently have him in the nurse's office."

Sally could only think of one thing as she put down her phone and took off for the school.

Since when did they have a *nurse's* office?

***

The twins were screaming up and down the hall with the other kindergarteners by the time Sally found her oldest son in the infirmary. He had removed his jacket and his distressed hat, his face pale and his overall demeanor sending Sally straight to his side.

"What in the world is wrong, huh?" She slammed her wrist against his forehead. No fever. "Do we need to take you to Dr. Meyer?"

She was informed that her son didn't have a fever, but had been complaining of an upset stomach. Paige screaming that she was "gonna kill" her twin brother wasn't helping Sally's headache. While the nurse took Paige aside and told her "*we don't say those things to our siblings,*" Sally looked Tucker in the eye and asked, "This isn't an excuse to go home early and eat candy, is it? You're not just excited about Halloween, are you?"

"Mom..." he said with a disbelieving scoff, "I'm missing out on the party in my class this afternoon. You know what that means? No prizes for the games."

"Yes, I heard Ms. Sutter went all out for the party this year," the secretary said. "Bobbing for apples and pin-the-boo-on-the-ghost."

"Sounds like what they're doing at the hall tonight," Sally said.

"Only I would get more prizes since it's a smaller class!" Tucker wailed.

"All right, all right." Sally helped her son up from his chair. "Let's get you guys home."

She had that sinking feeling that there was something Tucker wasn't telling her. *Call it my motherly intuition.* Sally took one look at her son and realized there was a story beneath that pale complexion. Somehow, she doubted he was legitimately sick. Not with the crud, or from something he ate, anyway. *He's got anxiety.* Sally saw it in his inability to meet her gaze and the way he clamped his mouth shut the whole ride home. This was a kid who often couldn't shut up about how his day went, and he wasn't above out-shouting his siblings if it meant his mom heard him first. Tack on the fact it was

Halloween and he was missing a big party in his class...

What in the world was he so anxious about?

Sally knew better than to prod him about it. Besides, she was busy with Paige and Gage, both of whom wouldn't settle down for their afternoon naps they would sorely need if they were to go to the party tonight *and* get up for school in the morning. On the rare occasion Tucker was home at this time of day, he often kept to himself and let his mom do her chores. Today, however, he was the saddest zombie-cop in the room wherever they went.

"You can put your costume back on *later*," Sally reassured her daughter. "Right now I need you to put your head down and close your eyes. I don't care if you think naps are stupid! You can stop taking naps when you're in first grade! Until then, it's nap time!"

"Mom?" Sally heard her son's pathetic plea for attention, but she was too busy checking in on Daisy's nap that she almost didn't register his words. "Mom?" He followed her into the next room, where she slammed down into an armchair and took a well-deserved break. "Mom?"

"What is it, Tuck?"

He stared at her for a few seconds. "Nothing. I'm gonna go lie down, too."

Sally should have been thankful for the peace and quiet she got for one whole hour. Instead, she listened to the silence and wondered when the other shoe would finally drop.

***

Paige and Gage tore up the American Legion Hall as soon as they arrived, their costumes instant hits with every teen and adult in the room. Sally barely had the chance to send Tucker off to have fun with his friends from school before other parents were asking how she painted the Captain America shield or got Paige's hair to flow like that beneath the Wonder Woman crown. When she told them her daughter was wearing a wig, they did a double take.

That wig was soon on the floor, however, since Paige was so excited to bob for apples she dunked her whole head into the tub. Cindy Smith, the woman in charge of the game, was quick to yank the wig off Paige's head before it contaminated the tub. Sally picked it up, brushed the debris off, and told her daughter she'd hold onto it until it was time for the contest. With her head free to be the way it was born, Paige raced down the aisle of games and prizes.

"The last thing that girl needs is more sugar." Sally turned to Tucker, who was still attached to her hip. "Well? Are any of your friends here?" Usually, this boy separated from his crazy family for some quality game time with his friends. "Or do you still not feel well?"

"My stomach hurts a little..."

Sally put a reassuring hand on his head. "If you really don't feel good later, let me know and I'll let you sit in the car." They weren't going home until the twins entered the contest which, thankfully, was only in an hour. By then they would have their fill of the games and be ready for their *one* horror cartoon at home. And by "horror" Sally meant a *Peanuts* Halloween special. They could eat their candy corn to tales of the Great Pumpkin. The end.

Tucker eventually saw a small group of friends and joined them in the rest area, which was a meager five-by-five space of folding chairs and a single table. One of his friends had brought a Switch and regaled his friends with whatever game he had brought from home. *Guess I should scrounge up some candy for him later.* No way were the twins sharing, and Sally didn't count on there being candy outside the door when they returned home.

"Hey, Sal!" She nearly leaped out of her skin when she saw Mayor Karen Rath waltzing toward her. Neither of her children were young enough for this event, but as mayor, she probably thought it pertinent to make an appearance. Either that, or she wanted to show off her Cleopatra costume. *Isn't that the same one you wore a couple years ago?* Someone had lost weight. "Been a while! Since I saw *you*, anyway. I see Candace all the time... anyway, how are you doing? Oh, my goodness, look how big this baby is! How old is she now?"

"Little over a year." Sally thought herself clever with her and Daisy's costume. The black witch's costume couldn't hide the orange blob attached to her torso. Daisy was half-asleep against Mom's chest, but that only made her more adorable – and more likely to be mistaken as Sally the Witch's pet pumpkin she carried around with her. Everyone who had seen her so far had commented how cute they both were.

"My goodness! Time really flies. Next thing you know, I'll be up for reelection." Chuckling, Karen gently touched Sally's shoulder. "Where are your other kids? I hope they're enjoying the fun. We kinda went all out this year."

She said that the moment another group of grade-school kids burst through the doors, their haggard parents stumbling in behind them. "They're around here somewhere," Sally said. "Not sure about Tucker, but the twins keep reappearing to ask me for another bag to put candy in. You'd think they were squirrels stocking up for the winter."

"I remember when my son was like that..." Karen said, referring to her oldest child, Xander. *He's in college now, right?* Sally could barely keep up with the aging of other people's children when hers kept her preoccupied enough. "Christina was never much into Halloween. Half surprised you don't have her babysitting this little nugget here so you can have some fun of your own tonight."

"It's all right. We won't be out too late at this rate, and you know how Halloween is... Candace will be working late, so it's better for me to get home, anyway. I need to make sure she'll have hot water to use and a warm meal to eat after God-knows-what happens tonight."

Karen nodded with appreciative understanding. "I've raised two teenagers. I know what they get up to."

They parted soon after, Sally to track down her twins and Karen off to hobnob with other members of their town. It didn't take long for Sally to find Paige shooting Nerf balls into hoops and earning candy while Gage played Avengers with an Iron Man and a Thor. She took a little pride in that her son's costume was the only homemade – and well made, thank you – of the bunch. The Iron Man and Thor came straight from a factory. Sure, they looked nice, but they didn't look *great*. Bless their parents for trying, though.

Gage slammed his hand-painted shield onto the floor and posed as if he had single-handedly reversed Thanos' handywork. Unfortunately for him, Iron Man was frightened of the noise and knocked over Thor. Soon, two six-year-old boys were crying and their parents came rushing forward.

"Gage!" Sally snapped. "Remember what I said about throwing? You almost hurt him."

She didn't recognize the kid playing Iron Man. She did, however, recognize his mom as someone who made PTA meetings a pain in the butt.

"Your son almost killed mine!" Greta Williams, dressed as Ray-of-Light era Madonna, bleated like a goat. "Dangit, Sally!"

The kerfuffle between parents drowned out the cry of alarm ringing behind Sally. It didn't help that Daisy soon started crying from all the commotion. *At least it gives me an out.* While Greta demanded an apology from Gage, Sally grabbed him and hauled him to the restroom where she intended to calm down her baby and settle her own nerves.

Instead, she found her oldest son and one of his friends. They were huddled over the older boy's phone, their foreheads knocked together and voices low.

"Well! Looks like a busy bathroom!" Sally waved to Tucker's friend, who shoved his phone beneath his costume. He rushed out of the room before Sally had the chance to ask him his name or what he was dressed up as. "Mind if your family uses the facilities, Tuck?"

He looked at her as if common sense no longer existed. The poor boy, with his pale face and shrugging shoulders, crawled off the plastic chair in the corner of the bathroom and acted like he was about to follow his friend into the other room. Didn't bother Sally any. She was busy with a crying baby and a six-year-old boy who still wanted to kick Thanos' ass.

"Mom," Tucker said as Sally lowered the diaper changing table. "I need to talk to you."

Daisy was still crying when Sally removed most of the pumpkin costume and thanked God it wasn't soiled. Not like the diaper which, again, made her thankful it wasn't as bad as it could have been. "What is it? Oh, would you mind looking after your brother over there? He really thinks he's Captain America."

Tucker didn't get any closer to Gage, who kept to himself in the far corner. He occasionally punched the wall or made explosion sounds with his mouth, but for the most part, he didn't need *minding. He needs a sedative.* Tucker needed something to perk him up.

"It's really important," Tucker muttered. "Something bad is gonna happen."

Sally looked up from her daughter's naked bottom. "Excuse me? Don't do that to me. Remember the story of the boy who cried..."

"I'm serious, Mom!" Tucker slammed his hands against the changing table. Daisy gurgled in apprehension. Gage turned around from his corner. "Some kids are gonna set fire to the city hall!"

Sally slowly turned her torso toward her son, whose cheeks were so red they faded through the pale vampire makeup on his face. "What was that?" she asked.

"Give me your phone and I'll show you."

She gestured for him to grab it out of her purse. *First, I need to get this diaper on my baby.* Then, she needed to grab Gage and have a talk with him about getting too excited while in costume. By the time she gave Tucker her undivided attention, he was sitting in the plastic chair with his face glued to his mother's phone.

"Here." He showed her a web-based chatroom. A popup asking her to download the app – which would be faster, easier to navigate, and *more secure* – appeared every few seconds, but Tucker continued to X out of it until his mother saw the conversation.

"PV City Hall," the highlighted message said. *"Eight thirty. Place should be clear as the security guard goes on break. It's gonna be LIT."*

"What in the world does this mean, Tuck?" Sally strapped her baby to her torso and held Gage's hand. That didn't give her much room for looking at her phone, but when Tucker looked at her like that, she was inclined to listen. "You involved with these people?"

"No! Some kids at school were showing me. I'm scared, Mom. Are they really gonna light the city hall on fire?"

How was Sally supposed to know? She barely knew what "lit" meant in this context. *I have long accepted that I am no longer hip with youthful lingo, but this would be a good time to suddenly become fluent, huh?* "You tell me! You're the one wrapped up in this!"

"I'm *not,* Mom! I only know about it!"

"You're only now saying something?"

"I didn't know that... I didn't want to be..."

The boy's bottom lip wibbled. Soon, the tears arrived, his whole body shuddering as he turned away from his mother and held himself to the bathroom wall.

Great. He wasn't going to be much help. Sally looked down at her phone again, scrolling through the conversation. Lots of abbreviations. Lots of acronyms. So much slang that she didn't know if this was still English.

But one thing was fairly clear. There were some kids in Paradise Valley talking about lighting the city hall on fire. If that wasn't a red flag, Sally didn't know what was!

"All right, let's go." She shoved her phone in her purse, looped the strap over her shoulder, and grabbed Tucker. "Party is over. We're going to get your other mom."

If there was ever a time for Candace to step up into her role? This was it! The time was now!

Chapter 16

CANDACE

The worst thing about Halloween was not having the chance to join her family in their dress-up festivities. Yet Candace knew that would be a sacrifice when she started having kids. *Missing out on one or two holidays a year is worth it for something like this.* She still got Thanksgiving, Christmas, and most birthdays. She still got to see her kids in their Easter best running after eggs and chomping on chocolate bunnies. Aside from Halloween, the only holiday that really took her away from the family was Independence Day because, like Halloween, it was when idiots ran amok.

If there was one thing she was hired to do, it was keep those amok weirdos in check!

"Tell me again, Sam," she said to the middle-aged man in lockup. "Tell me how many drinks you've had."

"Oh, well..." Sam burped into his mitten. Even without the noxious gas in the air, Candace could smell the alcohol all over him. *Literally. He spilled it all over himself when Peterson pulled him over.* The sheriff came by long enough to put the guy in lockup and have Candace babysit him. Which meant filling out the report for her boss, too. *Can't decide which job is worse, honestly.* "Only two. Lite beers. Hardly anything in them, you know?"

"Which is why you were swerving all over the road and can't touch your nose, right?"

"Yes, ma'am."

Sighing, Candace returned to her desk and stared at the form. That was a mighty high blood alcohol level...

Did this beat dealing with toilet paperers? Not really. Did this beat the kids trespassing into the old auto lot and doing some "artistic" graffiti? Nope. Honestly, Candace would rather be out there right now instead of staying in here until around midnight, when most of the town went to sleep on Halloween. *At least I get to come in later tomorrow.* And she got some mighty fine overtime for her troubles tonight. That would go straight into the Christmas coffers. The kids were getting old enough when most of their toys cost more than ever before.

Candace expected to see a couple crazy things that night, sure, but she definitely did not anticipate seeing the family car barreling into the parking lot and her whole family spilling out in costumed bliss.

"Everyone inside, let's go!" Sally swung the door open and motioned for her three older kids to get their asses into the waiting area. "That's right. All of you. You too, Wonder Woman."

Paige's wig was on sideways. Both her and Gage complained that they were missing the costume contest.

"To what do I owe this lovely pleasure?" Candace stood up from her desk and welcomed a barrel hug from her twins. Ah, almost. Paige initially missed her target since she couldn't see where she was going. "Honey, you've got your hair on all wrong. You're gonna hurt yourself." Candace attempted to fix Wonder Woman's wig, but it wasn't happening. "Aren't you guys supposed to be at the American Legion Hall?"

Sally motioned for her wife to come to her. When Candace peeled her twins off her legs and crossed the room, it was to pleas that Paige and Gage be allowed to play with the pens sprawled across her desk. While Candace didn't explicitly give them permission, she didn't tell them no, either.

"What's up?" Candace asked her wife. "Something wrong?"

"Yeah. I think something might be wrong." Before Candace could express her fear that one of the children needed the hospital, Sally shoved her phone in her wife's face. "Tucker showed this to me earlier. He says that some kids are planning something bad for tonight."

"What in the..." Candace snatched the phone out of Sally's hand and scrolled through some conversation. *I don't get technology very well, but I know some mischief when I see it.* "What is this? They're talking about Paradise Valley?"

Sally turned to Tucker, who looked to the floor. "Tell your other mom what you've been telling me."

Tucker looked up at Candace long enough to wipe some old tears from his eyes. "That's a chatroom for a bunch of kids who like fire stuff. I think they might be connected to the barn fires, but I don't know for sure!"

"Tell her about what that message from tonight says."

"It's... gonna..." Tucker choked on his words.

"Breathe, son." Candace knelt down on one knee, hand on her son's shoulder. "Take it slow, and tell me what they're gonna do."

He swallowed a lump in his throat. Naturally, it gave him the hiccups. The violent kind that knocked a kid on his ass if he weren't careful. "Some kids have come in from the city. They say they're gonna light city hall on fire, and they're telling people when to come by to watch."

"City... hall?" Candace looked up at Sally, who shrugged. "You sure about this?"

"That's what it says. Happening at eight-thirty."

Candace glanced at the clock. It was ten after eight, and city hall was a few blocks away.

"Shit." As soon as the kids giggled at their mom's cussin', Candace grabbed her radio and told Peterson. "I'm gonna go check it out," she said. "Meet me there if you can."

"Are you crazy? If there's a real..."

"I'll inform the firehouse we have a credible threat." Like the sheriff's office, the firefighters were pulling a long shift that night. At least every other year there was a sizable fire *somewhere* on Halloween, not to mention the medical problems everyone and their dogs had that time of year.

Candace turned to her wife. "Get the kids home. It's far enough away from city hall."

"Don't you do something stupid, Candy." Sally grabbed her wife's arm before she walked by. "What about that guy in there?"

"You fine back there by yourself, Sam?" Candace called.

"Never better, deputy!" he called back.

"He's fine. I've gotta go. You guys have gotta go home." Candace kissed her wife on the cheek and grabbed her jacket. "Save some candy for me, would ya? I'm gonna need it."

She knew what would happen if she stayed behind and suffered the consequences. Sally would beg her to stay behind and to not go by herself into the Halloween night. *If I had been listening to her since I swapped careers, I would still be slinging slop at the high school. She'd be working a job so we could afford a tiny two-bedroom house and we'd be lucky to afford one of our kids.* Everything they had was possible because Candace dared to follow her gut several years ago. She hadn't made it this far on luck alone. It had been fate. Like she chose to believe Sally was fate. Their kids were fate. Finding out about a possible fire that night was *fate.*

Because city hall wasn't a random target out in the middle of nowhere. It meant business. *I know for a fact that security guard works the place at night.* Poor Joe Roberts was a nice guy who made some extra money sitting in the city hall for most of the night. Every once in a while a few high school kids got drunk or high enough to try to tag the place with spray paint. Or some angry constituent threw a bottle at a window. Maybe someone with something to hide attempted to break in, but that was rare. *The point is that one man sitting around is enough to deter bad ideas. Most of the time.* What time was the arson supposed to happen? Eight-thirty. Hm. That was around the time Joe took a break, wasn't it?

Shit. This was thought out well, if true.

Candace hopped into the cruiser but declined to turn on the lights and siren. She wanted to catch the little bastards in the act instead of merely scaring them off. *If they have anything to do with the barn arsons, then I want them in custody.* Rumor had finally spread that Dillon Musgrave wasn't acting alone. The people wanted an end to the fires, yes, but they wanted those responsible to be held more accountable. Ever since that giant Columbia Gorge fire two years ago, wherein a teenager set off a firework during a burn ban and ignited one of the worst wildfires in recent history, people had been hesitant to let these things off the hook. It didn't matter how old the culprits were or how sorry they felt. If they endangered one innocent life, hell was to pay.

At least if I get there first, I control the situation. That's what Candace told herself as she drove down a backstreet and utilized the cover of darkness to hide her intentions from a small group of teenage boys sneaking around the back of the city hall.

Oh, she saw them. When she did, her shoulders hunched and her eyes narrowed in fury. Until then, it hadn't been *real*. It was still rumor. Hearsay. A possible false alarm, which would require her having a stern talk with her son. At least it meant nobody was using her town as a playfield for fire and smoke. What was worse? Having a troublemaking, wolf-crying son? Or having a small team of kids heading out to cause more than a little mischief

– they might kill someone, never mind the millions of dollars in property damages!

There was no time to sit back and think about what to do. Candace wasn't afforded the luxury of forming a game plan. The only way this ended was with immediate action. It was her vs. three... no, four, because that was definitely a shadow moving in the corner... teenagers that looked *awfully* familiar now that she was a little closer.

Oh, yes, I recognize you four. Hadn't they been in a car together recently? Speeding down *her* highway? Hiding something in the backseat that she naively took to be something like pot or alcohol and not, oh, accelerants?

She killed the engine at the end of the street. Damn door squeaked, though, so she had to be careful getting out and closing the door again. Candace stayed low to the ground as she cut from the sidewalk and passed through a small gap in the bushes lining the city hall's property. Old tape marked the spots for the biweekly farmer's market in the parking lot. What a lovely reminder that she had more than a building – and possibly others – to save. She had the town's history standing before her. She had a cultural landmark that served more than one function.

No pressure.

She radioed Peterson once more. He told her to stay put, which she agreed to do if it was safe enough. Since she was in the vicinity of the potential culprits, Peterson said he would radio the firehouse to be on standby. After that, Candace was on her own until either Peterson arrived in fifteen minutes or the kids skedaddled on their own.

"Something this big needs an accelerant, dude," the boy closest to Candace, a whole five yards away, said. "It's not an old, dry barn that will go down on its own. If we light the thing on fire, it'll barely make a dent before everyone shows up to put it out, and what's the point in that? We promised people a show!"

To prove how dumb these kids were, one of them whipped out his cell phone and took a selfie. "We're going live as soon as the spectacle starts," he said.

One of the kids returned from the car parked on the same backstreet Candace had used. She was grateful she had parked the clearly marked cruiser a ways away. Hopefully, they wouldn't see it. Especially since that kid brought with him a big red can of gasoline. *Let me guess. That was either in their trunk or hidden beneath a pile of bags in the back seat when I pulled them over.* Candace didn't have time to beat herself up about it. The could haves, would haves, and should haves would serve as a reminder for future situations. For now, she needed to keep on her toes and prevent a catastrophe. That meant focusing. That meant not thinking about her own safety – too much – or what might happen should this oncoming fire get so out of control that her own family was endangered. The Greenhills' house was a good half mile away. How quickly could something like this travel, though? There was enough wind that night an ember might fly to Florida Street and land on Sally's head.

No, no, Candace couldn't think about that. She had to focus. *Focus.*

"Accelerants are for wusses," one of the boys, perhaps the driver of the car, said. "Screw that noise. I say we hurry up and get those rose bushes over on the corner. They'll make nice kindling. Should jump straight to the front of the building, too, and we'll have a *great* show."

"You think Dill will see it from his house?"

"He doesn't live in this town," someone said with a snort. "So, doubt it."

"Still, we should do it for him. Our first bro to get taken down by the pigs. Come on, speaking of pigs, we need to do this before they get here."

Too late for that. Candace wasn't waiting any longer. These kids didn't look armed. Pocketknives, maybe, but no firearms. Still, Candace needed to be careful. There were four of them, and they weren't literal children. Not to mention... they had gas, and matches, probably. Candace didn't want either coming in her direction. Depending on how freaked out they got, this might end badly. For all of them.

One of the boys looked defiantly at the other and uncapped the gasoline can. While the others begged him to reconsider – not because it was the thing to do, but the *optics,* man! – he dumped some liquid on the nearest rose bush. *It's now or never, woman. Get your ass in gear!*

"Freeze!" Candace leaped out of the bushes, her gun drawn and her stance wide. She was already a large enough woman to make some grown men cower. How would four teen boys feel? "Hands in the air! All of you!"

With a yelp that echoed across Main Street, three out of four boys put their hands up. The only one who didn't was the one with the gasoline can.

"Put down the can, son," Candace said. "It's over. There are more cops on the way and the firehouse is right behind them." Maybe that last part wasn't true, but they would be at the word *go.* "Let's head down the station and have a little chat about what's going on here."

That last kid was not going down without a fight. *Maybe the driver isn't the ringleader, after all.* Damnit. Candace had two options. She could try tackling the kid before he lit a match.

But the kid with a phone had it on *her* now. Was he livestreaming? Lovely. No matter what Candace did, she was screwed.

What was more important, though? Keeping her job, or keeping people safe?

She wasn't the type to shoot unless she felt she was in mortal danger. So she lowered her gun and attempted to show good faith. Not that it got her anywhere. Two seconds later, the kid dumped the can and pulled out a lighter from his front sweatshirt pocket.

Here went nothing.

Candace slammed into him, her heavy body tackling his to the ground. There was enough gasoline still in the can that it sprinkled across her jacket and hat, the smell so profound that Candace nearly gagged. The other kids split up and ran in different directions. They probably would have gotten away, too, if it weren't for the Sheriff's car pulling up along Main Street.

"Where the hell do you think you kids are going?" Peterson didn't have to pull out his gun. One kid collapsed into a frightened fit of tears while the others took off in the same direction.

Another deputy vehicle swung in front of them. Nobody was going anywhere.

Including Candace, who was still on top of a kid who futilely beat against her shoulders. Not until Peterson approached did Candace finally get up and confiscate the lighter.

Peterson chuckled. "Up to some wild mischief tonight, aren't you, son?"

Although this surely meant Candace wouldn't get home until five in the morning, she couldn't help but beam in pride. Not because of what *she* did, but because it meant another night her kids got to sleep in peace.

Chapter 17

SALLY

The concept of "downtime" was a foreign one in the Greenhill household. There was always something to do. Someone needed cleaning up. Something needed to be cooked. And, God forbid, someone might need to go to the doctor because for the third time in as many months, they swallowed something they shouldn't have. (That someone's name was Gage, of course. Wait. Wasn't it Paige that one time? Sally couldn't keep track any longer.)

Yet sometimes the stars aligned and Sally was gifted a relatively low-key day with her wife by her side, helping to manage the kids and make sure everyone didn't collectively walk out into traffic while playing Frisbee in the front yard.

Veteran's Day happened to be the last hurrah of decent weather. Everyone was bundled up in sweaters, but the air was warm and there was no sharp breeze. Candace had woken up that Monday morning, still on work time although she had the day off, and decided it was a good chance to barbecue one last time before putting the grill and charcoal away until Memorial Day. *When did these government holidays focusing on the military and patriotism become about making hamburgers and hot dogs in your backyard?* Oh, if Sally thought long enough, she'd notice the correlation between a precious day off and spending time with one's family. When she had four kids underfoot and a wife preoccupied with cooking, however, she didn't have time to flesh out her shower thought.

"More vegetables for you." Sally deposited a bowl of freshly cut vegetables next to the grill, which smoked with flavorful promises – as long as Candace didn't get ahead of herself with throwing every seasoning she found onto the meat. *Last time she did that, my stomach was upset for a week.* "How's the meat coming along?"

"Hot dogs are about ready. Burgers are right behind them. How about the fries?"

"If by fries you mean tater tots, yes, they're in the oven."

"Tater tots, huh?"

"You heard the kids in the store. As soon as I pulled the bag of frozen fries out of the freezer, they were yelling about tater tots."

"I mean, to be fair, tater tots are pretty great."

Sally contained the eyeroll threatening to pop her eyeballs out of their sockets. "I'm starving. Looking forward to this mess."

"Speaking of mess, has Tucker calmed down after that phone call earlier?"

There was another thing Sally didn't want to think about. Her oldest was now embroiled in the arson investigation, thanks to his confession to his mother about what he had seen online.

While he wasn't in trouble, he was young and sensitive enough that a brief interrogation over the phone, was enough to send him up to his room for a few hours. So happened that the last phone call came while he was playing Frisbee with the twins. Candace had intercepted the call, demanding why the Portland detectives were calling on a federal holiday. She was brusquely informed that not everyone is allowed to take holidays off. Like that meant anything!

Since then, Tucker sequestered himself in his room. With the early dinner nearing its completion, Sally was inclined to go upstairs and ask him to come down and help her set the table. *It may be nice looking outside, but like hell we're eating out there! Too cold!* Instead, she opened all the blinds and curtains in the living room, inviting what was left of the afternoon sunlight into her house.

"Haven't seen him." Sally nudged her wife. "Don't worry about it. I'll take care of it."

"I feel bad for the kid, you know." Candace shook her head. She made room for the raw vegetables on the grill and threw some asparagus – that only she and Sally would eat – in with the meat. "He did the right thing, and now he must feel like he's being punished for it."

Sally rubbed the small of her wife's back. "He did the right thing because he's got such a strong role model in you. He knows how to tell the truth and when to speak up. He idolizes you."

Candace blushed. She'd probably pass it off as the smoke touching her cheeks. "People always say he likes to walk like me. Though, I kinda hope he doesn't want to be a cop one day."

"He'll definitely be helping people, regardless of what he does. By the way, is it true that the investigation has been handed over to Multnomah County?"

"Right now it's a joint investigation, since most of their targets started around here. That's all I can really say about it." Candace snorted. "Yeah, right. Give it another month. By Christmas, the Portland and Gresham folks will be breathing down our necks to hand over everything we have."

Sally assured her that wouldn't happen, although she knew better. Many of the crimes committed by the minors (and few adults) happened around Paradise Valley, yes. but there were also arsons in the Willamette and Rogue River Valleys that were attributed to the online group promoting arson in the Pacific Northwest. The FBI would get involved sooner rather than later. *Maybe then I'll have Candy back...* Sally knew that was a selfish thought. Candace had one of the most important jobs in the community. Because of her, those kids had been caught before they lit the city hall on fire! Because of her actions, she was having her own commendation dinner at the American Legion Hall shortly after Thanksgiving. Mayor Rath had personally come down the street to tell Candace the news. *"It's the least we can do,"* Karen had said.

Honestly, Sally could think of a few other things the local government could have done besides a commendation, but she wouldn't say anything. She would be happy enough to put this all behind them and go back to being a family.

She talked Tucker into coming downstairs and setting the table. The baby was already in her highchair, and the twins finished their latest round of whatever video game they played. Sally had placed the plates down on the table when Candace entered with a stack of cooked meats and vegetables.

Chaos ruled over dinner, but Sally didn't mind. Her children were loud, their utensils clanging against plates and minor ice water spills blotching the white tablecloth. Candace's already booming voice had to reach new heights to be heard over her own children. A hot dog bun flew across the table and landed on the windowsill, much to the delight of Daisy, who clapped her hands and exclaimed something that sounded like, *"Again! Again!"* Gage, who had snuck the TV remote to the table, turned it on with full volume, scaring the food out of Sally's mouth. Yet before she had the chance to take the remote away from him, Candace gave him one stern look and held out her hand in parental anticipation.

Sally lost count of the number of tater tots that ended up on the dining room floor. She didn't know how many times Candace asked their children to settle down and eat their dinners. Nor did Sally know how long it took them to make it through their courses and start thinking about bath time.

She got up to change Daisy's diaper. Candace held up her hand and said she would do it. While she didn't offer to also do the dishes, having Candace take over children duty allowed Sally enough time to gather up the dirty plates and wash them in peace. Without having to worry about who went into the tub first and who needed a diaper change, she didn't have to also rush through her other chores. Why, she could stand in front of the sink and enjoy the sunset!

Imagine that!

"Baby's changed and in her crib," Candace announced forty-five minutes later. "Tucker's reading a book on the couch, and the twins are in the bath. Don't worry about them. I'll check in later to make sure they haven't given the floor a bath as well. How are the dishes? You finish them? Oh, I better go put the grill away. Hey, when I get back, let's have some popcorn for dessert and watch some TV. Have we cracked open that DVD of 'Toy Story 4' yet?"

Sally could hardly believe her ears. She only had to do *one* chore? Candace was offering to do more?

I knew she always wanted to be more active around the house, but... Sally couldn't remember the last time she got a bit of a break. It had to have been... June? Maybe June. Back before the fires started and Candace sold her soul to the investigation that frustrated her more than anything else.

This is what I've always envisioned... Her family sitting together around the dinner table and enjoying a movie before the kids had to go to bed. Laughing and cuddling and simply living in the moment. Watching the kids yawn and finally pass out in chairs and on the carpet. One by one they went up to their rooms to get some extra sleep before school the next day. As for Sally? She stayed put on the couch, picking popcorn out from between the cushions and preparing to take the dirty bowl to the couch. Yet before she could get up, Candace appeared and asked if they should watch something more suited for adults.

Sally also fell asleep on the couch, with her head propped up on Candace's shoulder and a blanket flung over her body. She didn't remember going to bed. For all she knew, Candace had carried her. It wouldn't be the first time – but certainly the first time in a good, long while.

Sally woke up the next day more refreshed than ever, and convinced that the best of their marriage was still to come.

October Twilight

Hildred Billings is a Japanese and Religious Studies graduate who has spent her entire life knowing she would write for a living someday. She has lived in Japan a total of three times in three different locations, from the heights of the Japanese alps to the hectic Tokyo suburbs, with a life in Shikoku somewhere in there too. When she's not writing, however, she spends most of her time talking about Asian pop music, cats, and bad 80's fantasy movies with anyone who will listen...or not.

Her writing centers around themes of redemption, sexuality, and death, sometimes all at once. Although she enjoys writing in the genre of fantasy the most, she strives to show as much reality as possible through her characters and situations, since she's a furious realist herself.

Currently, Hildred lives in Oregon with her girlfriend, with dreams of maybe having a cat around someday.

Connect with Hildred on any of the following:

Website: http://www.hildred-billings.com
Twitter: http://twitter.com/hildred
Facebook: http://facebook.com/authorhildredbillings
Tumblr: http://tumblr.com/hildred

Made in the USA
Thornton, CO
09/04/24 19:31:08

1dc69323-3021-4d08-a8cd-6abbd5797f78R01